KU-350-333

Other Manning Coles titles available from
Carroll & Graf:

MANNING COLES
COLES
ALL THAT
GLITTERS

Carroll & Graf Publishers, Inc.
New York

CONTENTS

The room was not large but bare to austerity; there was a roll-top bureau in the middle; a substantial safe in one corner, and a draughtsman's desk, like a wide sloping shelf, along one wall; there were two or three wooden chairs and, over the windows, heavy curtains, the residue of wartime black-out. There were four men in the room. Two of them were at the bureau which had been forced open; they were pulling out drawers, emptying their contents upon the floor, and hunting through pigeonholes. A third man was staring gloomily at the safe and the fourth was merely standing in a corner looking unhappy. The man by the safe turned his head sharply.

"Listen! Someone coming."

In the silence which followed there came clearly the sound of loose slippers descending an uncarpeted stair.

"Put that light out."

"It's the old chap himself," said the man in the corner.

"If he comes in, Ackie, hit him with the cosh. No shooting."

When the room was dark a bright line under the door showed that the lights had been switched on in the hall outside. The footsteps drew near the door; it opened and showed against the light the figure of a man in pyjamas. He peered into the darkened room and set his hand upon the electric-light switch. At that moment Ackie struck and he fell heavily, switching on the light as he did so, and lay face downwards across the threshold.

"Well, thanks for turning the light on, anyway. These bureaux are all much alike; there's an alleged secret compartment in most of them. Which of these little drawers is shorter than the others?"

"You've killed him," said the man in the corner, and crept across towards the doorway.

"Nonsense. I didn't hit him hard enough. Besides, he's breathing."

"This drawer. Now, there should be a spring here somewhere—ah."

There was a sharp click and an inner compartment slid forward; it contained only a long slim key with a turreted barrel. The finder took it out and said "Ah" again, in a satisfied voice, and carried it across to the safe.

"I don't like seeing him like this," said the man from the corner, kneeling beside the unconscious body on the floor. "He wasn't a bad old stick."

"You are a fool," said the man with the key. "Always were and always will be." He pressed the key into the lock, turned it right round and withdrew it, then turned the handle, and the safe door swung open.

"It is not really clear to me," said Thomas Elphinstone Hambledon, "why they should have asked for me in the first place, why you should want me to go merely because they have, and what the plague I am supposed to do when I get there."

"In the first place," said the spokesman for the Foreign Secretary persuasively, "they have asked for you because they want you. Don't let's use that tiresome and indefinite 'they'; the application for your services was put forward by the Bonn government at the instance of a Mr. Spelmann whom I believe you know."

"Heinrich Spelmann? Oh yes, I know him. We worked together when I was in Cologne two years ago. He was a private detective in those days, though I do remember hearing that he was later taken on by the Security people at Bonn. That was under the Allied administration, of course. Is he working now for the West German government?"

"Certainly he is, and holding quite a good position."

"Oh, really," said Hambledon. "Glad to hear it; he had abilities and was certainly a hard worker. But I

6

still don't know why he wants me there. This aircraft designer fellow what's-his-name——"

"Renzow. Gustav Renzow."

"Renzow, thank you—hears noises in the night, comes down in his pyjamas to find a burglar or burglars in the act of breaking into his safe, and gets banged on the head so effectively that he's been unconscious ever since. The burglars got away with his personal papers—passport and so on—and a set of drawings for an aeroplane which is alleged to be of no particular value. And, presumably, any loose cash there may have been lying about. Spelmann, no doubt, was told to go and look into the matter because there were some aircraft designs involved. Well, he doesn't want me, he wants a reasonably bright specimen of the Bonn police force, plain-clothes division. I may be getting a bit grizzled," said Tommy, delicately stroking his temples, "but I am not yet in my dotage. You don't send me galloping about Europe to do jobs which would be far better done by the local police. Come off it. What is all this?"

"It's on the border of the French zone."

"Well?"

"And the French are not satisfied that it is all as simple as it seems."

"It has never been easy," said Tommy, "to satisfy the French."

"No. On the other hand, if a French detective were to be sent up, it wouldn't satisfy the Germans."

Hambledon laughed.

"So you see," said his friend, "why it is that when Mr. Spelmann successfully urged the Bonn government to apply for you, the French backed the application."

"I see that far," said Hambledon, "but still not why your crowd granted the request."

"We are always anxious to assist the French whenever it is reasonably possible and we are particularly anxious to oblige them at the moment."

"Oh, ah."

"For reasons which I should prefer not to mention."

"Please don't trouble," said Hambledon politely. "I can read the newspapers for myself."

"Well, there you are. Hambledon, what is all this fuss about? You like Germany and you always enjoy going there. I agree that it doesn't look as though this is your job, but why worry? Go over and show willing, drink the local wines and talk to the local people, encourage Mr. Spelmann in his endeavours, and have a good time generally. He will be pleased, the French will be gratified, and you will be happy. When you get bored you can come home again. Well?"

"I see. I am to be a bone of contentment and an apple of concord. All right, I'll play."

When Hambledon arrived at Wahn, which is the airport for Cologne and district, he saw a man he knew among the group of people who had come to meet their friends. Heinrich Spelmann had not changed in the least since Hambledon had last seen him two years earlier; he was still a short square man who habitually went hatless, with a mop of white hair blowing round his head like a halo whenever there was the least wind. He still wore a disreputable waterproof and his square sunburnt face was eager as ever. Hambledon greeted him with genuine pleasure.

"It is delightful to see you," said Spelmann, "quite delightful. I was, frankly, a little afraid that you might refuse to come. This matter, you would say, is for the police, why bother me? Let us walk this way. I have a taxi waiting outside the Customs. So it seems, this affair, a matter for the police, and if it turns out to be so at least we shall have met again and you can sit on a terrace above the Rhine with a glass on the table before you and talk to everyone you meet, can you not? It will be a holiday."

"Yes," said Hambledon, "yes. I am delighted to have the opportunity of spending a few days with you and, to be frank, that is why I am here. What I have heard so far about this case does not suggest that I can be of much use to you. However, perhaps there is more in it than appears on the surface."

"I think so," said Spelmann with emphasis.

Hambledon passed the Customs and rejoined Spelmann, who said that he had taken a room at an hotel at Königswinter for Hambledon. "We will drive straight there now, if you agree; it is only twenty-five kilometres and we shall arrive in time for dinner."

"Königswinter—I ought to remember——"

"It is just above Bonn. It is one of those little Rhine towns, on the right bank between Beuel and Bad Honnef; Mehlem, where the American Headquarters are, is just opposite."

"Oh, is it?" said Hambledon in a tone of surprise. "I thought that was the French zone, across the river."

"Not just there. The zoned boundary is just upriver from Mehlem. Rolandswerth is in the French zone."

"And Königswinter?"

"British, up to the other side of Bad Honnef. Look," said Spelmann, digging into the poacher's pocket of his raincoat, "here is a map. A large-scale map, it shows the boundaries."

Hambledon looked at the map. "I wonder why on earth these zonal boundaries had to be so irregular; they twist about like a drunk snake. The French zonal boundary goes up the middle of the Rhine for about three kilometres. Why didn't they just rule off straight lines on a map?"

Spelmann shrugged his shoulders. "Who knows? Not that it matters as between the British, the Americans, and the French; there is no check, control, or hindrance of any kind upon their boundaries. It is only the Russians who are different; you must be careful with the Russians."

"So I hear," said Hambledon drily. "How far off are the Russians? I see. About two hundred kilometres."

"Not nearly far enough," said Spelmann sourly.

"Oh, I agree. But far enough to prevent my straying accidentally into it if I walk in my sleep. Now tell me, why are we going to Königswinter?"

9

"Because it is where Renzow lives."

"Oh, is it? I see. But what do you suppose I can do there? You do not suppose his assailants are townspeople, do you?"

"No," said Spelmann, "but one must start somewhere. As for what you can do there, it is a charming place. It is just at the foot of the Drachenfels. It has an ancient church and numerous ancient winehouses where you can try the local vintages and talk to the people. When you are tired of that you can walk in the *Nachtigallenwaldchen* and listen to the nightingales which St. Bernard chased away from Heisterbach because they disturbed his prayers. You can—here is the Lorelei Hotel, and no doubt dinner is served."

"You will dine with me, Spelmann, will you not?"

"I thank the Herr. I shall be honoured and delighted."

"A glass of wine in the lounge before we dine," said Hambledon when Spelmann had swept up the porter, the desk clerk, and the headwaiter and more or less cast them at his visitor's feet. "You know, it's very odd how saints dislike nightingales. There is a district in my own country called St. Leonard's Forest where there are many sorts of birds but no nightingales. St. Leonard told them to go away for the same reason as St. Bernard's. What will you have?"

"A little glass of Moselle, if I may?"

"And you a Rhinelander! Certainly. Waiter!"

"The Moselle wines are lighter," said Spelmann almost apologetically. "These nightingales, they sing all night of love, so the poets tell us, do they not?"

"And you think the saints understood what they were saying?"

"Being saints, no doubt they had supernatural attributes?"

"Oh, probably. Of course, that would account for their telling the birds to go away. I can't think of anything more disconcerting to a saint. About this fellow Renzow——"

10

"After dinner," said Spelmann hastily, "after dinner I will tell you all about it."

"You will remember," said Spelmann, comfortably settled in a far corner of the lounge with Hambledon beside him and coffee before them, "that after the war was over there was a manifest desire on the part of the Allies to secure the services of distinguished German technicians in various branches of science and industry."

"Call it a hectic scramble to grab them before the Russians got hold of them, and vice versa."

"Yes, yes indeed. It was like that. Gustav Renzow was a draughtsman in the Focke-Wulf works at Bremen before the war and proved to be a young man with ideas. You do not want his autobiography. Towards the end of the war he was one of their foremost designers, though no longer at Bremen. He is a Rhinelander. This house at Königswinter was his father's; at the very end he was living here and working at an aircraft factory at Bassenheim, near Coblentz. When that stopped work he merely remained at home."

"Most of these technicians left Germany and went to America or Russia as the case may be. Why did he stay here? On account of the nightingales?"

"He refused to leave," said Spelmann pointedly, "and that, my friend, is one of the reasons why I think that there is something behind all this. He was offered a most desirable post in America and he declined it. Why?"

"A typical Nordic blonde, possibly? Is he married?"

"No. He had a sister whose husband was a Nazi of high rank in the Party. He was killed in Berlin at the end. Her daughter, Anna Knipe, is Renzow's housekeeper and secretary. She lives with him; her mother died long ago. I have interrogated her several times and she is keeping something back. I know it, I can feel it here." Spelmann patted his chest. "You have read the official reports of the case?"

11

"Not the full reports, a précis only. His safe was broken into, he came downstairs——"

"The safe was not broken into; it was unlocked with its own key. The key was kept in a roll-top writing bureau which was kept locked, and it was this that was broken open in order to find the key of the safe."

"Someone knew where he kept it," said Hambledon.

"Certainly, the Herr is right. Fingerprints show that there was more than one man in that room that night, probably three. Only one print is good enough to photograph and that has not yet been identified, though we have not—that is, the police have not yet received replies from all the several places which keep criminal records."

"Several men. You mean several strange fingerprints, don't you? Any real reason to believe that they were all men? And were they necessarily all burglars? Could not some of them be those of visitors since I understand that Renzow is still unconscious and cannot answer questions?"

"His niece says there were no visitors and her statement is corroborated by their servant. Moreover, that room was his office, where he worked; if he had visitors they would be received in one of the two sitting rooms."

"Unless, presumably, the visitors came on business. And are you sure the niece and the servant are telling the truth? Didn't they hear anything that night?"

"No, but their bedrooms are at the other side of the house. As for the visitors, if there were any, why should they deny it? It is not a crime to have visitors."

"Spelmann, Spelmann," said Hambledon reproachfully, "this is unworthy of you. It all depends upon who the visitors were. Have you tried your fingerprints upon the records of the Security people? This man Renzow was a Nazi, was he not?"

"I tried the Security records first of all, but without result. Yes, he was a Nazi, but he had to be in order to hold the position he did hold. He was not an enthusiastic member."

12

"They all say that," said Tommy in a bored voice, "just as everyone in the occupied territories now tells you he was in the Resistance. But I keep on interrupting you. They broke open a roll-top desk, took out the safe key, and opened the safe. What is missing?"

"They took his personal identity papers, and a passport which had recently been issued to him, and a set of drawings—designs—a design—for an aeroplane. His niece told me that the design was not particularly valuable because under test the wing had shown a fatal weakness. However, the design was considered by the Americans to be so interesting that Renzow was being encouraged to overcome the difficulty."

"Oh. Was that all they took? Personal papers, a passport, and a dud aeroplane design?"

Spelmann cocked his head on one side and looked at Hambledon. "You do not believe it either?"

"Well, they might have been just unlucky," said Hambledon reasonably. "I suppose burglars do draw blank sometimes. One thing I refuse to believe, and that is that they broke in to get his passport. I wonder they bothered to take it; it's much simpler to get a faked one."

"Yes. It is a very large safe," said Spelmann slowly. "It is as big as a household refrigerator. It was made in Bonn and I went to see the makers. They remembered all about it very clearly. It was requisitioned from them in February 1945 by an Army officer. They were very pleased to make the sale because at that time, only two months before the end of the war, they thought that nobody would ever want a safe again."

"Having nothing to put in it."

"Exactly. They thought it a little odd that anybody should want to buy a safe when already the guns of the Allies could be heard like summer thunder in the distance and drawing nearer every day. However, the officer requisitioned it and brought an Army lorry to transport it. Having no employees left except a couple of cripples, the partners went out on the lorry to Königswinter and installed it themselves. When they asked for payment they were told it would be sent in a day or two, but in point of fact the money was not sent. They showed me the requisition order; it was signed by August-Ernst Knipe, General. Renzow's brother-in-law."

"Who was killed in Berlin some six weeks later, you said."

"That is right."

"One intriguing point about this mystery, to my mind," began Hambledon.

"Yes?"

"Why didn't the Bonn firm take their safe away again when they weren't paid for it?"

"I make no progress," said Spelmann sadly, "in convincing you that there is anything in my story. Renzow paid for the safe ultimately. Why, mein Herr? To keep, as you say, his passport in? If he did not want it, why not send it back? If he did, what did he keep in it?"

"And what did General Knipe get it for in the first place?"

"I asked that question of his daughter, Anna Knipe, Renzow's niece. She said that she did not know. She was not at Königswinter at that time; she was nursing the wounded. She did not see her father at that time; indeed, she never saw him again. She said that no doubt he installed it for some purpose and was possibly prevented from carrying the purpose out, whatever it was."

"Yes, that is quite likely, but it doesn't explain why Renzow paid for it instead of sending it back. What did he want it for, as you asked just now?"

"To keep his designs in, she says."

"And you don't believe her," said Hambledon.

"No, mein Herr. Because Renzow paid for it in January 1948, and he did not take up his aircraft work again until the middle of 1950. He had a clerk's job in the Municipal Gas Office in Bonn."

"Did you point that out to her?"

"No, I checked the dates since I last saw her. In any case, she was lying. She is a nice woman, really," said Spelmann reflectively. "She ought to be married and have

14

several happy, healthy children. She is not unpleasantly clever; she is domesticated and wholesome to look at. She is naturally truthful, and it is as plain as sunlight when she is speaking the truth and when she is not, but you cannot shake her. I would stake a good deal that the secret, whatever it is, of why the safe was bought and what was kept in it is not a disgraceful one. She lies and she does it badly, having no natural gifts that way, but she is not ashamed of doing it. Rather the contrary."

"Some sort of trust," suggested Hambledon, and Spelmann nodded. "Yet she is not anxious to help you to recover whatever was taken."

"It might be something which they would not be allowed to keep if it were known that they had it."

Hambledon leaned back in his chair and smiled at his old friend.

"For the first time since I arrived, there is a faint suggestion that I may find something else to do here besides enjoying your company."

Spelmann's face lit up and he sprang to his feet. "That is what I have been praying to hear you say! There is a mystery here and we will unravel it, you and I." He began to walk up and down across the corner of the lounge where they sat; the room had emptied until there was no one besides themselves in it except a loving couple holding hands in a far corner who did not even look round. "All this time I have been afraid that you would say: 'Call in your police, Spelmann—thanks for your company—good-bye.' Now we work together again, you shall advise me and I will help you. I have an office now, Herr Hambledon; I always told you I would have a real office one day and not a converted bedroom such as I had in Cologne two years ago. I have men under me and access to official files. All these things delight me afresh every morning when I wake up, but the real crown of my success is to be able to say to the Bonn authorities: 'Entreat my friend, the famous Herr Hambledon, to give me the benefit of his advice,' and here you are. This it is," said Spelmann, swinging round at each turn of his quarter-decking so that his white hair swirled round his head, "this it is to work hard and be successful. What will you have with me? Waiter! I hope they have something you will like. Waiter! Have you any Grand Marnier? Two Grand Marniers, please. Ha!"

2 SHAREHOLDERS' MEETING

Hambledon was sitting in the sunshine at a table by an open window overlooking the busy Rhine and finishing his breakfast of coffee, rolls, and butter, when Spelmann came into the room. The little detective's face was bright, his step jaunty, and his manner that of the bearer of good news.

"You have brought me luck," he said. "I knew you would. You are without doubt my better half."

"Your—— Oh, I see. Glad to hear it. Have some coffee and tell me all about it."

"Thank you, just one cup. In the first place, the police have been diligently enquiring of everyone in Königswinter, Bad Honnef, Dollendorf, and the neighbourhood whether anyone was about that night and whether they saw anyone. They found at last a forester whose child was taken ill and who had walked into Königswinter to fetch the doctor. He passed by Renzow's house at a little before two in the morning. Just before he reached it a car drove up to the house and stopped in the road outside. Only side lamps were left on and by their light he saw four men turn in at the gate and walk up to the house. There is a short path to the door. The forester came back a quarter of an hour later with the doctor in his car. The car which had stopped was still there and even as they passed a light came on in the fanlight over the front door."

"Renzow coming downstairs," said Hambledon.

"So I think, also."

16

"He can't tell you anything about the car?"

"Nothing, except that it was a saloon car, not an open tourer. Besides, he says he was not interested, the child was choking. However, he is quite definite that there were no lights visible at the house until the hall light went on, but the visitors might have been in some room at the back. Why not?"

"Four men," said Hambledon.

"And that is not all my news. The Berlin—Western sector, naturally—police report that the one identifiable fingerprint is that of Bruno Gruiter, a Berliner who has already served two sentences for burglary. They telephoned this to the chief of police in Bonn this morning; I happened to be with him when the call came through. They said that they would send us particulars of him, photographs and so forth. Our chief asked them whether they would make a search for him and they laughed at the idea. I heard it myself, squeaky noises from the telephone receiver. They asked whether anything of immense value was missing and our chief had to say that it had not been clearly established what was missing but that a householder had been brutally assaulted and was dangerously ill. They laughed again and said it was too bad, but in Berlin murder was a commonplace and stolen goods there were not petty valuables but living men and women. Our chief apologized for troubling them; I heard him do so and I should have done the same in his place."

"Yes," said Hambledon, "yes. So should I. Have your police interviewed the doctor?"

"Not yet. He had started out on his rounds by the time they had got the forester's statement. He has a big district; he starts early and will not be home before lunch."

The Königswinter doctor was a large elderly man with grizzled eyebrows which stuck out. He gave his visitors a glass of wine, poured out one for himself, and lit a pipe which had a china bowl decorated with pink roses.

17

"Of course I remember the occasion," he said, "but the car I saw could not have brought the miscreants who hammered poor Renzow. It was a French staff car, I saw it distinctly. I noticed it with surprise and then the obvious explanation struck me. Renzow's house is a little outside the town—you have seen it? Yes. It is quiet and private there. If a car stops beside a country road in the small hours the occupants are probably returning from a party. No, I did not mention it to the police. Why should I? The French occupation troops are human like the rest of us. I thought nothing more about it."

"But the forester had seen the car stop there when he passed on his way to your house a quarter of an hour earlier. Four men got out and went up to the house."

"Oh, indeed? He did not tell me that. Are you sure it was the same car?"

"The forester thought so," said Spelmann. "Also, lights went on in the house at the moment when you were passing."

"Oh, did they?" said the doctor. "I did not notice that. I shouldn't, you know, if they came on just as we were passing; I should be looking ahead. Renzow is one of my patients; in fact, I was called in when they found him in the morning. I packed him off to Bonn. A depressed fracture of the skull is not a thing which the local medico attempts to treat in his surgery. Dear me, no. I do not wish to be arrested on a murder charge. And rightly. I rang up the hospital and they sent out an ambulance for him and I understand that they operated the same day. That is now four days ago. Has he recovered consciousness yet, do you know?"

"Not by nine o'clock this morning. Can you tell us anything about the car?"

"Only that it was a French staff car with the usual markings on it. It was a Citroën, I think. I didn't notice the number, I'm afraid. Probably the French authorities can help you, though I still think my explanation much more likely. The car poor old Rupprecht saw probably went off again; it wouldn't have taken them long to break open that desk and open the safe with a key. The fact that the car I saw stopped in the same place was, in my opinion, coincidence."

"Any idea what he kept in that safe?" asked Hambledon, speaking for the first time.

"My dear sir! I have not the slightest idea. His drawings, presumably. I never saw it until the other morning. I had not been in that room before."

They took their leave and drove back to Bonn. Spelmann went away to telephone the French authorities to ask if they had lost a staff car on the night when Renzow's house was broken into. He came back an hour later to say that they had indeed lost a car that night; it was taken from one of the official parks at Bonn. Its movements had been traced for most of its journey that night; it had passed through Königswinter, going South, at about 2 A.M. and returned half an hour later. It was not noticed in Bonn. "But it wouldn't be," said Spelmann. "Why should it? There are so many. It was seen again passing through Hersel on the road to Cologne and has not been seen since, although the British have made the most searching enquiries."

Hambledon lifted his shoulders. "Sprayed a different colour, with fresh number plates and a set of impeccable papers," he said, "it could be in Amsterdam, Brussels, or Paris long before this."

"Or Rome," agreed Spelmann gloomily. "Or Madrid."

"Or Constantinople," said Tommy briskly. "I beg the Turks' pardon, Istanbul. This discussion is profitless. I think I shall go to Berlin. I used to have a lot of disreputable friends there and perhaps the police will spare a moment from their more pressing cares to tell us who Gruiter's associates are. If they know. Are you coming?"

On the second day after the robbery at Königswinter four men sat round a table in a semi-basement room in the Western sector of Berlin. The room was gloomy although the sun was shining outside; it had once formed part of the storerooms of a large department

19

store, now in ruins, but this lower part of the building had been strongly built, being part of the foundations of the five storeys above. These semi-cellars had been cleared out, cleaned, subdivided into living accommodations, and let to the homeless. Some of the rooms had very little furniture of any kind and others far too much, according to whether the tenants had been able to salvage any of their possessions or not. This one was overcrowded but reasonably clean; Hans Ackermann's wife had been house-proud when she had had a house of which to be proud. She was out at that time. Acker-mann had sent her out because the four men had private matters to discuss; otherwise they would probably have been sitting round a table in a café in the sunshine. One of them was Bruno Gruiter, who had carelessly left his fingerprints in Renzow's office at Königswinter when Hans Ackermann had attacked the designer; the third was named Andreas Claussen, and the fourth Karl Edberg. Claussen had been standing by Renzow's safe while Gruiter and Ackermann were hunting through the desk for the key; Edberg was the man in the corner who had shown some humane feeling when Renzow had been struck down. He referred to it again.

"I suppose the old chap isn't dead," he said. "There's been no mention in the papers."

"Of course not," said Ackermann. "I told you at the time I didn't hit him hard enough."

"That don't worry me," said Claussen, "half so much as having to leave all them stones parked like that."

"They're all right," said Gruiter, "and what we've brought away's enough to go on with. We couldn't bring it all with us, could we? All through the Russian zone on that lorry?"

"We was hung with 'orseshoes," said Edberg, "gettin' through like that. Them Russians didn't hardly look at us, seemed 'alf asleep or something."

"Well, why should they?" said Gruiter. "One 'eavy lorry loaded with iron girders in the middle of a convoy of seven 'eavy lorries loaded with iron girders, why should

20

they look? Them loads come up and down that road all day and all night. I told you we'd be all right, and Aug filled up the forms for us, didn't he? Wind up, that's what you had, Ed."

"Them Russians," said Edberg, "give me the 'orrors."

"Bilge," said Gruiter contemptuously. "They can be bluffed like anyone else. Easier. They're slow, they are. Look at Bart Lachmann, he ain't afraid of 'em."

"He's smart," said Ackermann, "Bart Lachmann is."

"I saw him this morning," said Gruiter. "Wanted to know how we'd got on."

"Got on?" said Claussen. "What does he know? You didn't tell 'im anythink?"

"What d'you take me for? He knew we'd been away. What d'you expect me to tell him? We'd been to a spa for our rheumatics? I told him we'd come across some designs, looked good to me. Parts of aeroplanes or some such." Gruiter smiled slowly. "That Bart, he'd sell flea powder to a flea. Said he'd come and look at 'em."

"He knows about that sort of stuff," said Edberg. "Worked in a drawing office at a tank factory in the war."

"Why weren't he in the Army?" asked Claussen.

"He was, for six weeks," said Gruiter. "Then his heart went back on him, so he said, and the doctors believed it. I reckon he knew a chemist, myself."

Claussen, once a front-line soldier, snorted, but the others laughed.

"What does he reckon to do with the drawings when he's seen 'em?" asked Edberg.

"Sell 'em to the Russians," said Gruiter, "if he thinks 'em good enough to pass. They'll buy anything that looks like Western scientific stuff, he says."

"Anythink Renzow thought up 'ud be good," said Edberg. "Real top-notcher, he is, in his line."

"That's right. I asked Bart to come along," said Gruiter, "and we'd show him. Might see if he's outside now, will you, Ackie?"

Ackermann went out and came back five minutes

21

later with a thin dark man in the early thirties who might have been good-looking if his eyes had not been too near together. His suit was shabby and threadbare but well cut, his shirt had been carefully darned, and he wore a clean collar and a neat tie. He looked like a bank cashier or a junior partner in an architect's office, and his manners were easy and friendly. He greeted Edberg and Gruiter, was introduced to Claussen, and sat down at the table.

"Quite a board meeting," he said pleasantly. "The Chairman will now take the Chair and address the shareholders."

Gruiter said that he had already told Lachmann that they had come into possession of some designer's drawings of what appeared to be an aeroplane though it looked rather a funny one to him. He had never seen an aeroplane with a wing anything like that but he was no expert and didn't pretend to be.

Lachmann said that he also was no aeronautical engineer but he did know something about engineers' drawings. Perhaps the gentlemen would care to let him look at them.

Gruiter looked round the table; Ackermann and Edberg nodded and Claussen said: "I suppose so," in a surly voice. Ackermann got up and opened the bottom drawer of a chest of drawers which appeared to be Frau Ackermann's linen press, for he lifted out sheets and towels to extract from below them some large sheets of tracing linen which had been folded up small instead of being rolled.

"Sorry they're creased like this," said Gruiter. "We had to fold 'em up small to carry them on us."

"Doesn't matter," said Lachmann, unfolding the first one handed to him, "they'll iron out if necessary. Ah."

The first sheet, as it happened, was the general arrangement and showed an aeroplane with swept-back wings, the wings being hinged in such a way as to make it possible to vary, in flight, their angle of sweep. So much the notes at the foot made clear, though why

22

the designer should have gone to all that trouble was an insoluble mystery to the uninstructed round the table. The other sheets made clear the means by which the alteration in angle was to be effected. Each sheet was signed in the corner, G. Renzow.

"I don't know in the least what all this is about," said Lachmann frankly, "but if this doesn't lift the Russkis right off the seats of their chairs, I'm a little baby Hottentot."

"Besides," said Edberg, "I expect they'll have heard of Renzow."

"Of course," said Lachmann. "You can bet on that. Why, even I have heard his distinguished name. He's famous. Oh, they'll know all about him." He examined the sheets again and read the marginal notes. "It would be nice to know what all this is about," he went on. "What is a 'high maximum lift coefficient'? Don't all speak at once. Oh well, it doesn't matter, I haven't got to know. I'm only the vendor."

"I take it," said Gruiter, "that you think these drawings are worth money to the Russkis. Are you prepared to undertake to sell them?"

"I thought I'd just said so," said Lachmann.

"I only wanted to make sure. All right, then. How do we set about it?"

"They won't see these, of course," said Lachmann. "They will only see photostats of just enough to show them what it is but not how it works. I think each photostat should be of the bottom right-hand corner of each of these sheets, say a quarter of each sheet, but including the designer's signature in each case. Then I go across to the Russian zone and tell them the tale. I must get to see some real expert—and they have some, boys, make no mistake about that—because only a real top-liner would know what this design is worth. Or understand it, for that matter. I mean, some Russian Air Force bod would be worse than useless. This design will stay here in the meantime. Not necessarily here," he added, glancing round the room, "I mean, in your care;

23

I was thinking particularly of the risk of fire. These sheets"—he flicked them with his finger—"are not the sort of thing to attract a casual thief who didn't know anything about them. Not like precious stones, for instance. Stones won't burn but, by heck, these will. Fire is a great cleanser," said Lachmann sententiously, "but we don't want it cleaning these up. I leave all that to you. Then we must arrange for some foolproof method of getting the money in exchange for the design, and no monkey business; that'll want some thinking out. If I want the design brought across the frontier to meet me, will one of you do it?"

"Not me," said Edberg instantly.

"I don't mind," said Gruiter. "I'm not afraid of them."

"That's the spirit."

"How much?" asked Ackermann.

"I shall require notice of that question," said Lachmann, smiling. "We shan't get what this design will be worth to them because they'll know very well that we can't sell it anywhere else. So it's what they offer us or nothing. On the other hand, if they want it they will want it at once, and we can, if we choose, keep them waiting for months. If they want it they will pay, no doubt about that. It's just to strike a balance."

"You mean, a bargain," said Gruiter, and Lachmann laughed.

"But you must 'ave some figure in your mind," persisted Ackermann.

"We shall be lucky," said Lachmann, "if we get three hundred thousand marks. Western marks, of course."

"Well, that'll do, divided up," said Gruiter comfortably. "A man can live on——"

"And the division," cut in Lachmann, "will be half to me and the rest between you four."

"Too much," said Claussen, speaking at last. "You didn't get 'em."

"And you can't sell 'em," said Lachmann bluntly.

"One third," began Ackermann.

24

"Half, or I walk out here and now," said Lachmann. "And I've seen the design, remember."

"Was you thinking," said Claussen ominously, "that there'll be a reward out for these drawings?"

Gruiter intervened hastily. "It's plain idiotic to start quarrelling about the divvy-up before we've started selling the goods. All the same," he added in a plaintive voice to make the others laugh, "I think if I risk my neck going into Russia I ought to get a bit more myself."

"I agree," said Lachmann cheerfully. "Look, I'll make a concession. If Gruiter does come he shall have a slice off my half. But I'm going to have half or I don't play. Well?"

"I agree," said Edberg. "They take the risk, don't they?"

"Oh, all right," said Ackermann.

"Claussen?" said Lachmann.

"Too much," said Andreas Claussen, but he moved uneasily.

"Three to one against you, Anders," said Gruiter persuasively. "Come on."

"Oh, very well, since you're all against me. Western marks, mind."

"Thank you," said Lachmann. "Thank you, one an' all. Western marks, certainly. Now, there is one other thing. How are we going to finance this trip? It'll cost money."

"We've talked that over," said Gruiter, "already. You must keep the cost down, but anything reasonable we'll find."

"Splendid," said Lachmann. "You are gentlemen a man can work with. Now, does anybody know a photographer? Because, if not, I do."

3 THE FERRET

On the following morning Lachmann came to the room where Ackermann lived and found Gruiter also there.

25

"I've spoken to my photographer friend," said Lachmann casually. "If you'll let me have the sheets I'll just pop around and get them done."

"Certainly," said Ackermann. "I'll come with you, me and Gruiter. I'd better carry them and you an' Bruno can be bodyguard. You're both quicker in the uptake than what I am, if there was to be any sort of trouble."

Lachmann knew perfectly well that all this was merely a polite cover for the fact that none of them would trust him with the sheets out of their sight, and he did not resent it. A reasonable precaution; he would have done the same himself. They would come into the photographer's studio too, talking cheerfully about how interesting it was to watch a skilled man on his job, but it would be only to make sure that nothing more than the agreed portions were photographed. He was quite right, they did. It turned out that Gruiter had been something of a photographer in his better days before the war and his comments were intelligent and instructed. Ackermann merely watched closely and in silence; when the business was over he and Gruiter took the designs away again.

The next day the photostats were finished and very well done. Lachmann showed them to his four fellow shareholders and received from them an agreed sum of money, Renzow's passport (suitably adapted), and other evidences of identity from Renzow's desk.

"Listen," he said. "I've been thinking about how to get the money in exchange for those drawings and no chance of any monkey business with those Russkis. When the price has been agreed, they'll send a man with the money. I mean, they won't just give it to me, I'm afraid."

The others laughed and Lachmann with them.

"I'll travel back with him and take him to Gruiter's place. The designs will not be there. I don't mind where you keep 'em, boys, but they must not be in the room I bring the man to. Then, when we've seen the money all present an' correct, Gruiter will go and fetch those sheets from wherever you have kept 'em while I and the Russki wait together. When Bruno comes back, we will swop the sheets for the money. O.K.?"

The men nodded.

"Any amendments?"

Ackermann leaned forward.

"It do seem a pity," he said, "to let them papers go when the money's there and us two to one against the Russki. Or even three to one to make sure; I could come back with Bruno."

But Lachmann disagreed energetically. "No, no, that wouldn't do at all. Look, you might want to do business with these bods again one day, and what would happen then? 'Sides, we don't all want to leave Berlin, and what would our lives be worth if we'd done the like of that, with them all round us 'ere?"

Edberg supported him. "We don't want them after us," he said, and shivered.

They settled a few more details, including a message about the date and the time, and Lachmann said goodbye. He started upon his journey at about the time when Hambledon arrived in Berlin; Gruiter, Ackermann, Edberg, and Claussen had nothing to do but wait for the prearranged message.

Hambledon went to Berlin by himself; Spelmann was a busy man with other cases claiming his attention in Bonn. He could follow Hambledon to Berlin at any time if matters became interesting or exciting and Hambledon thought that he was more likely to gain his ends by strolling inconspicuously about by himself. Spelmann was a noticeable figure, easily remembered, readily recognizable and becoming quite well known. Some of the people whom Hambledon wanted to meet were of the sort who just naturally disappear round corners when they see anything resembling police; if they saw Spelmann they would probably leave the city.

Hambledon came to Berlin by air four days after his arrival at Königswinter; even for him it had taken some time to obtain permits and passes to enter Berlin and a seat in an aeroplane. This aircraft was circling the Tempelhof airport while Lachmann, straphanging in an underground railway train, was passing from the Western sector of Berlin into the Russian zone with a set of photostats in his wallet. Hambledon went straight to his hotel; his bedroom was small, dark, and inconvenient and overlooked acres of dismal ruins where the rats fought and squealed at night, but he knew that he was lucky to have a room to himself and made no complaint. His first call was upon the Berlin police, among whom he had some friends.

They were very pleased to see him and said so; they asked him out to dinner—to wine parties—to their clubs. They asked after old so-and-so and where was what's-his-name now and then their eyes turned unwillingly to the piles of work on their desks.

"But I am not entirely on holiday," said Hambledon. "If you could spare some junior clerk for ten minutes to look up a little information for me—thank you so much. I am sorry to be such an infernal pest——"

He explained that what he wanted was any information about one Bruno Gruiter who, he understood, was on the records. His address, his associates, his habits, whether he was in Berlin at the moment, and anything else they knew.

"Bruno Gruiter," said one of them. "Somebody sent us his dabs the other day—I remember. The Bonn police. They said he'd broken into a house and clouted the householder on the head. Why, has he died?"

"Not so far as I know," said Hambledon.

"I asked if he'd got away with anything and they didn't seem to know."

"He got away with some aeroplane designs and the householder he clouted was Gustav Renzow."

"Oh. The devil he was! Well, now, come along to Records and they shall be laid before you, such as they are. Also, I'll give you a note to the district police station of the area where he used to live and they'll be able to give you a good deal more, I daresay. I don't suppose he lives there now, though."

Records and the local police station told Hambledon quite a lot. Bruno Gruiter, aged forty-two, unmarried, born in Berlin of German parents, was apprenticed to a cabinetmaker and later worked in a furniture factory until the war, when he was called up and served with the artillery. He returned to Berlin on the cessation of hostilities and was convicted in 1948 of breaking into a house in American occupation and stealing cutlery, table silver, some small ornaments, and a silver cigarette box. "He forced the latch of the dining-room window and just swiped what he could find," explained the sergeant in charge of this section of Records. "He was heard and the occupier of the house came down and chased him. An American officer. Unfortunately for Gruiter, the American was a crack quarter-miler and just ran Gruiter down. He got six months."

"He was unlucky, wasn't he?" said Hambledon. "If that didn't make him honest, nothing would."

It did not. In 1949 a German policeman off duty was saying good night to a girl in the shadow of some trees outside a house in the Moabit district when Gruiter came quietly from the back of the house. The policeman abruptly went on duty and Gruiter got two years that time.

From the district police station Hambledon received a more personal picture. Gruiter was not a bad fellow really and life was difficult for the poor in Berlin, as the Herr would understand. Gruiter had got into a bad set and a string of names followed.

"These men have not all been convicted or even arrested," said the superintendent of the district. "It is one thing to be morally sure that a certain man has done a certain job or, at the very least, knows more about it than he is telling, and quite another thing to be able to charge him with it. But no doubt I am telling the Herr what he already knows."

Hambledon nodded. "You get that in every country,"

he said. "At least, in every country where the police act in accordance with civilized rules. Is there anything you can tell me about any of these men?"

The superintendent called in for consultation such of his men as happened to be in the station. Melcher was a pick-pocket, but was not much esteemed. Claussen was a jewel thief, mainly from hotel bedrooms. He only took good stuff; he had been employed by a jeweller before the war and knew valuable stones when he saw them. Twedt stole from cars and Goldstein snatched handbags. Edberg was suspected of stealing a car or cars, but it had never been proved. He had been a chauffeur-batman in the war to a Nazi general named Knipe who——

"Named what?" said Hambledon sharply.

"Knipe. He was fighting against the Russians in Poland towards the end of the war; his lot fell back on Berlin and he was killed here in the last days."

"Any of you know what Edberg looks like?"

Apparently there was nothing particularly noticeable about Edberg and since he had never been arrested there was no official description or photograph. One of the police who knew him by sight described him in the police manner, but it was a description which could apply to a good many men of the ordinary blond, Germanic type. "Nothing remarkable about him at all," said the speaker, "except that he's said to be terrified of the Russians. Maybe he has reason."

Ackermann, Hans, aged thirty-six. Robbery from the person with or without violence. He joined the Hitler Youth movement and was one of its most active and energetic workers. The superintendent made a grimace. "I was a constable then," he said. "We were not, of course, permitted to interfere. Ackermann served in the Green Police. When the war was over he came home and I had the pleasure of dealing with him for a couple of offences. He has only just come out. A nasty thug."

"His wife is a decent woman," said one of the constables. "My wife knew her when they were children. She looks terrified now, my wife says."

Hambledon thanked them all with the utmost sincerity and came away, thinking chiefly of Karl Edberg. Chauffeur-batman to General Knipe, Renzow's brother-in-law, and all the way from Berlin to the Rhineland in order to burgle Renzow's house. It could be coincidence. All generals had batmen and most generals had brothers-in-law. An ex-batman might well fall into bad company and evil courses when his general's purifying influence had been removed, and if one of his acquaintances broke into the house of one of the late general's relatives, the ex-batman need not necessarily have had a hand in it. In fact, one might argue to the contrary. If the ex-batman had been fond of his general, his attitude might well be: "Leave my old man's family alone, can't you? Go and burgle somebody else."

On the other hand, Gruiter had made a long journey, right out of his own territory, to burgle Renzow's safe. Edberg could have been one of the party of four since only Gruiter's prints were clear enough for reproduction, and in any case, the police had not got Edberg's prints on record. Hambledon found it hard to believe that Gruiter would go all that way in order to steal a set of aircraft designs said to be of dubious value. Unless, of course, he had been commissioned to do so. Who said that the designs were faulty? Renzow's niece. How did she know? Did Renzow tell her, and if so, was it true?

Against this must be set Spelmann's account of how the safe was obtained. General Knipe had it installed. What for? Then he was killed. A safe like that is an expensive thing, but Renzow does not return it to the makers. On the contrary, he pays for it himself, and this two and a half years before he takes up designing again.

"What the hell," said Hambledon to a statueless plinth in the Tiergarten, "did Renzow keep in that safe?"

He walked on for nearly a mile, turning left and then right again and again but bearing generally southwards until he reached a street which, when he last saw it, had been almost all ruinous. The houses had been uninhabitable but the ground-floor shops had been either salvaged or small temporary premises put up within their shell, as often as not by the previous owner. Hambledon was looking for an old friend, a one-legged cobbler named Sachs, who was, only the previous year, working in one of these temporary shops. However, when Hambledon reached the spot he found that the whole block had been cleared away and was now barricaded off with six-foot hoardings from within which came the sounds of hammering, drilling, chipping, and industrious concrete mixers. Hambledon was at a loss. He paused, looking about him, and then began to walk about down one side turning and up the next, but there was no sign of Sachs.

Presently he noticed a red-haired boy whose noticeably grimy face peered at him out of a gutted building. Hambledon stopped and said: "Here. Come here, I want you."

"Not me," said the boy, preparing for flight. "What for?"

Hambledon grinned at him cheerfully.

"Do you know Sachs the cobbler? Used to work further back there?"

"Old Peg-leg? Oh yes, I know him."

"He's still about, is he?"

"Oh yes. He's only moved. He got turned out of there, so he went somewhere else."

"Do you know where?" The boy nodded. "Will you take me to him?"

"It'll cost you fifty pfennings, mister."

"That's all right."

The boy disappeared for a moment and then came out through a gaping doorway.

"It's some way," he said. "Near the railway."

They walked along together with the boy half a pace ahead and always, Hambledon felt, poised for flight. He was about fourteen, red-haired and freckled, dressed in an assortment of clothes, some of which were too big for him and some too small but all in reasonably good condition. In a city where so many people seemed dull and spiritless from undernourishment, he looked well fed, alert, and intelligent and his eyes were everywhere.

"What's your name?" asked Hambledon.

"Frett, they call me. Frettchen, you know."

Frettchen means a ferret and was obviously a nick-name.

"I mean your real name."

"I don't know," said the boy indifferently. "I've forgotten."

"But haven't you got any people?"

"People?"

"Belonging to you. Relations."

"Oh no. I remember when I was little being told that my father and mother were killed in a raid here in April 1941. I don't remember it; I expect I wasn't there. I do remember the woman who looked after me for a time after that, but she was killed in 'forty-three. I remember that all right; they dug me out and I ran away."

"How old were you then?"

"Oh, I don't know. About six, I suppose. There were a lot of us running around then; we used to pinch food and things and live in the ruins, then they used to round us up and put us in schools, but I always got away again. It wasn't a bad idea to be indoors in the winter, but I couldn't be shut in all the summer too. I can read," said Frett proudly, "and count and add up. When I knew that I didn't go back to school any more."

"But where do you live—haven't you got a home?"

"I've got a place of my own but I'm not telling anybody where it is. It's mine, I found it."

"How do you manage when you're ill?"

"I'm never ill."

"And do you darn your own clothes?" asked Hambledon, noticing the neatly repaired elbows on the boy's jumper.

"I get a woman to do that." Frett looked round at Hambledon with a slightly abashed smile. "She lets me have a bath on Saturdays in her washtub. I haven't got to, I just like it. It isn't sissy to like having a bath now and again, is it? Some of the fellows say it is."

"Certainly not," said Hambledon emphatically. "A man who is a man has a bath as often as he can; it's very low to let yourself go dirty."

Frett looked at him closely.

"I expect you have lots of baths, you look so clean. Every day?"

"Almost every day. Sometimes I have to miss it."

Frett lost interest. "That's where Sachs lives, across the road there. Now can I have my fifty pfennings?"

Hambledon gave him a mark.

"Oh, thank you! Thank you very much. If you want taking about again I'll do it."

"But where shall I find you?"

"Oh, I'm generally about."

"Well, good luck to you," said Hambledon, and crossed the road to the cobbler's shop, where Sachs sat upon a stool close to the window to make the most of the fading daylight. He spent the whole day there, bent over his work with his wooden leg straight out before him; apparently he only glanced up now and again but, in fact, very little escaped him, as Hambledon knew. He had hardly stepped off the pavement when Sachs saw him and his face lit up with pleasure; when Hambledon entered the shop he was warmly greeted.

"It is a good day that brings the Herr again," said Sachs, shaking him by the hand. "Come and sit on the stool I keep for my best customers and tell me all the news. I have had to move, as you see. I was swept out with the rest of the rubble from where I was before. Never mind, I am still alive and so is my wife. Things might be worse. How is it with the Herr?"

Hambledon sat down and gave Sachs some tobacco he had brought for him; after some time he introduced the subject of Gruiter.

"Poor Gruiter," said Sachs thoughtfully. "I can't help being sorry for him."

"Why?"

34

"He has taken up a new trade," said Sachs with a swift glance at his friend. "You know, perhaps? Yes, I see you do. He used to be a cabinetmaker. It is a pity he didn't stick to that; he was a good cabinetmaker."

Hambledon laughed. "I had heard that he had been a little unlucky."

"It is a mistake to take up a profession for which one has no natural gifts. The Herr is interested in Gruiter?"

"I should like a little chat with him," admitted Hambledon.

"If you could make him see how foolish he is it would be a good deed. I have not seen him about for some time now, two or three weeks, perhaps more. I heard that he had left the city with some friends of his and that they had gone to the West, but I don't know what for."

"Do you also happen to know the friends who went away with him?"

"Hans Ackermann was one. I know him as—how shall I put it?—as one knows a bad smell in a certain spot which one often passes. One forgets about it and then, as one draws near the spot, one is reminded of it and there it is. He is not a friend of mine."

"I gathered that he wasn't," said the amused Hambledon.

"Karl Edberg was another. I don't like him much but I have nothing against him. He has a good appearance and is well mannered, I think he was an officer's servant at one time. He is a good driver. I find him dull, but it may be because I can't talk about motors; the good God did not intend me for a mechanic. So I didn't become one. I have heard that the fourth was a man named Claussen but I know nothing about him."

"And have they all returned from their mysterious journey, have you heard?"

"I have not heard, no, but it is only fair to say that I have not asked. Gruiter—I have known him a long time as one knows so many people, but we were never intimate or even near neighbours. Has he, then, been in mischief, or am I indiscreet in asking?"

"He's been in something all right," said Hambledon with a laugh. "He left his fingerprints all over the place. That's between ourselves," he added.

"Certainly, certainly. I do not babble, as you know of old." Sachs clicked his tongue in an irritated manner. "That Gruiter, really! I thought every child knew about fingerprints by now. He should have stuck to his carpentry, I said so before."

"He certainly seems a singularly inefficient burglar," said Hambledon. "I shouldn't think he'd last long. As a burglar, I mean."

Sachs picked up his work again, filled his mouth with nails after the manner of cobblers, and went on resoling a boot.

"How did the Herr find me here?" he asked, indistinctly because of the nails.

"A boy brought me. Lad who calls himself Frett."

"That boy," said Sachs thoughtfully. "I sit and wonder sometimes what he'll be when he grows up. He makes more money now than most of us do."

"Good gracious! How?"

"Oh, one way and another."

"Has he got parents?"

"No. Nobody knows who he is or where his people are. He is one of the 'wild children'; most of them were rounded up and sent to schools by the Welfare people, as the Herr knows, but this one could never be persuaded to stay. No one knows where he lives or how he manages, but he does very well."

4 APPOINTMENT AT NINE

Hambledon came out of Sachs' shop and turned to go back to his hotel. Frett, who had been hanging about for no particular purpose, saw him go and strolled aimlessly towards the cobbler's with some idea of having a word with Sachs which might throw some light upon this unusual person who gave one a whole mark when one had only asked for half. Frett felt there was something about him which made one desire more of his company and it was not only the prospect of money. Curious.

Beside the cobbler's shop a narrow alley ran back between its flimsy side wall and a more solid building in reasonable repair. As Frett wandered past the end of the alley an arm shot out, a hand closed upon him and dragged him in. Frett turned like a wildcat, all teeth and claws, but the man who had seized him pacified him at once.

"All right, all right, I'm not a policeman. Want to earn some money?"

Fret left off struggling and asked what for. The man pushed him gently back to the corner.

"Look along the street there, that man in the grey suit. See the one I mean? He's waiting to cross the road."

Frett nodded.

"He wants to see a friend of mine; he was asking Sachs about him. There's five marks for you if you bring him to my house tomorrow night at nine."

"What d'you want him for? Ten marks, mister."

"I don't want him really, it's him as wants us."

"Then why didn't you stop him yourself?"

The man backed cautiously into the alley and took Frett with him.

"Because there's a policeman along there and I don't want him to spot me. See?"

Frett saw. The situation was familiar to him.

"D'you know me?" went on the man.

"I knows you. I don't know your name."

"That'll do. Know where I live?"

"In the middle one of them three houses behind where the brewery used to be."

"That's right. Bring him there tomorrow night at nine o'clock sharp and knock on the door like this." The man tapped on the wall three times, a pause, once, another pause, and then twice. "Three—one—two. Then I'll know it's you and not the police. Got it? You do it."

37

Frett obeyed correctly. "But I don't know where he lives."

"You cut along after him now, he's not hurrying. Follow him and see where he goes. When you bring him to my house there's five marks for you. Off you go."

"Ten marks," said Frett, merely moving out of reach, "or I don't go."

"You money-grubbing obstinate little blockhead, I haven't got ten marks," said the man in an exasperated voice. "Get on or you'll lose him."

"Seven marks, then. Your pal as wants to see him'll put up the other two."

"Oh, all right, all right, seven marks. Now get cracking or——"

But Frett had already gone. There was indeed only one direction in which Hambledon would be likely to go in order to reach the quarter where were situated the three or four hotels available to temporary visitors. Unless he were staying with friends he would go by this street or that and in any case cross a certain square—Frett took a short cut across some waste ground, running and leaping like the animal for which he was named. The chase was longer than he expected, for Hambledon had realized that he was hungry and mended his pace, but at last the grey suit and the English felt hat showed up under a lamp in Potsdamer Strasse; Frett sighed with relief and followed a little way behind. Hambledon paused at the door of his hotel to let some people come out and Frett ran up to him.

"I say, mister——"

"Hullo! You again?"

"I've got a message for you."

"What is it?"

Frett backed away to be out of earshot of the commissionaire and Hambledon followed him.

"A man stopped me and said as there was a man you wanted to see. That right?"

"Could be," admitted Hambledon. "If it's the right man. Did he give you a name?"

"No. Asked me if I knew his name and I said no, but it wasn't true, I did know."

"Well, what was his name?"

"Claussen."

Claussen, the jewel thief, the man whom Sachs had heard of but did not know, the friend of Gruiter.

"That right, mister?"

"Near enough. What about it?"

"What's it worth if I take you there? Ten marks?"

"Certainly not," said Hambledon. "Seven is quite enough."

It was a major event in Frett's career that for the first time in his life he did not argue the point.

"If I come here for you at half-past eight tomorrow night——" he began, but Hambledon interrupted him.

"Where is the place? Anywhere near Sachs'? Very well, I'll meet you by the bridge where the railway crosses the Potsdamer Strasse at nine."

"Too late, mister. We've got to be there at nine."

"Oh, he mentioned a time, did he? Very well, the bridge at a quarter to nine, then. By the way——"

"What, mister?"

"What are you having for supper tonight?"

Frett was so surprised that he actually blushed.

"Oh, I don't know——"

"Come with me," said Hambledon, and led the way to a café across the road, where he sat down at a table and ordered beer for himself and a plate of *Krostcher wärm* —a sort of stew—for Frett.

"Real meat," said Frett, round-eyed.

"Don't you get real meat as a rule?"

"Sometimes I do, but mostly it's sausage. Real meat costs money."

"Wind that into yourself," said Hambledon when the meat was served, and Frett attacked it in a manner which was almost savage. Hambledon lit a cigarette, drank his beer, and said nothing for a time; appetites are keen at fourteen. When Frett had cleaned up the plate so thoroughly that washing it would be merely a matter of routine, he pushed it back and looked across at Hambledon.

"I say, mister."

"Well?"

"Don't go tomorrow night."

"Why not?"

"They—I don't like that lot."

"Claussen and his friends? What d'you know about them?"

"Not much. I keep away. I only know one other." The boy's voice dropped.

"Who's he?"

"Ackie. That's what they call him. Ackie. You keep away, mister."

Ackermann, the ex-Green Policeman, the thug, Sachs' "bad smell."

"Listen," said Hambledon, leaning across the table. "You have been given an address to take me to, I suppose."

"It's the middle house behind where the brewery used to be," which conveyed nothing to Hambledon. "I've got to knock on the door like this, three-one-two," said Frett, tapping the table. "That's to prove it's us and not the police."

"Yes. Well, they won't do anything to me there. They won't dare, because you will know where I went. If I don't come out again reasonably soon you can go to the police, can't you, and tell—— Oh well," in reply to the look on Frett's face, "you can go and tell Sachs, he'll do the rest. I'll tell some friends of mine where I'm going before I start; that'll make it quite safe. Nobody attacks people who are known to have gone to their house, because they would be suspected at once. Do you follow that?"

Frett nodded, but his face showed that he was not convinced, so Hambledon added: "I'm not quite helpless myself, you know. I've dealt with roughnecks before. In any case, this has got to be done." He paused a moment. "Thanks all the same."

Frett gave it up.

Hambledon walked down the Potsdamer Strasse the following night. When he reached the place of meeting he looked about for the boy but did not see him. Tommy told himself that he should have known better; Frett was not of those who stand about under a light. Hambledon strolled on; when he passed a place where a shop front jutted out and cast a strip of shadow Frett was suddenly there at his side.

"That's right, mister. You—you are going, then?"

"Of course I'm going. Carry on."

Frett sniffed audibly but made no other protest. They turned right and walked into a district of small streets all much alike, a district which had been a confused muddle when Hambledon had known Berlin well but which was more confusing and more of a muddle than ever now that war damage had removed so many of the landmarks. In ten minutes he knew only that he was south of the Kurfürstendamm and walking roughly parallel to it and that Sachs' shop must be a couple of streets away on his left. Presently they came to a still-imposing entrance with the wreck of a large building inside.

"The brewery," said Frett.

"What a shame to smash it up, wasn't it? Much more useful as a going concern."

Frett glanced up at Hambledon's face; his expression was one of mild interest and even amusement, but the boy had noticed that Hambledon's right hand had been in his coat pocket ever since they had turned off the main street. The reason for this suddenly dawned on the boy.

"I say, mister!" in a thrilled whisper. "You got a gun?"

Hambledon's eyebrows went up but he only said that the time was getting on and how much further was it?

"Only jus' down here and round the corner. What's the time?"

Hambledon looked at his wrist watch by the light of one of the infrequent lamps.

"Two minutes to nine."

"Just about right."

41

The streets here were practically deserted; they were not such as anyone would loiter in for pleasure. They never had been even when they were populous, an unsavoury district in its best days. Hambledon's hand tightened upon the Luger automatic in his pocket and his thumb rested upon the safety catch.

"Down here," said Frett, and led the way into a lane running beside the brewery wall. The other side of the lane was occupied by small houses, most of them tenanted; there were lights in the windows and in one a gramophone was playing an American dance tune. Further along the lane a car was parked, heading towards them, and Hambledon noticed that it bore Eastern zone number plates.

Frett checked slightly. "I never saw a car down——" he began, when a door opened silently just beside them, there was a rush, and Hambledon found a cloth cast tightly about his face from behind and both his arms seized in a grip so paralyzing that he could not even release the safety catch on his gun. As he was dragged backwards into the house he felt rather than heard that Frett had left him abruptly and gone off like a startled cat.

Hambledon was manhandled along a short passage and into a room almost wholly dark; only a faintly lighter square showed where the window was. He was pushed against a wall and his hands tied behind him, rather incompetently tied since the operator was working in the dark and Hambledon knew how to hold his hands so that the binding was not nearly so tight as it appeared. The trick had been shown him by a professional escaper from bonds who had been one of the "turns" at the Portsmouth Empire years before. Tommy blessed his forgotten name and faced round upon his unseen assailants with more confidence than they would have believed, especially as they had taken away his automatic.

"Sure this is the right man?"

"Sure. Saw him come round the corner."

"You ought to've got Frett too," said a third voice.

"Tomorrow 'ull do for Frett. You go and get the car, Ed."

"Wait a few minutes," said the first voice, presumably Ed. It was rather a high-pitched voice with a tinge of nervousness in it. "Best make sure first no one noticed anything." Hambledon, working at the knot with the tips of his fingers, nearly thanked him. "Did he see you?"

"It won't matter in half an hour's time," said the second speaker, "whether he saw us or not. But no, he didn't."

"You can't knock him off here," said a fourth voice which had not previously been heard. "We've got the police knowin' too much about us already."

"Of course not. We'll take him into the Eastern zone; the Russkis won't worry. Nor report it, neither. What sort of a car you got, Ed?"

"American. Packard saloon. Got Eastern zone number plates. Took it for that reason. Shan't be stopped on the border."

Hambledon thought it time he took a hand.

"You don't suppose you'll get away with this, do you?" he said. "You mutton-headed thugs, the police know I came here to meet you."

"Oh no, they don't. Frett told you where you was to go, didn't he? Well, that ain't here, that's in the next street. When they finds your dead body, which may be tomorrow or may not be for a month, they can come and ask us. We're all sitting at 'ome waiting for you to come, we haven't been out all evening. In fact, we're beginning to get worried 'cause you don't come, aren't we, boys? We're afraid something must have happened. We've got witnesses to all that. That's what they call an alibi, in case you don't know."

The last knot came loose and Hambledon held the cord between his fingers and his hands clasped lightly together behind his back. It was dark in the room but not utterly dark; already he could see where the four men were, two sitting and two standing up. If they had been

43

in the dark for some time they might be able to see him fairly plainly.

"Go and get the car, Ed."

"All right," said the high-pitched voice. The man nearest the door went out, and silence fell on the party. Hambledon had no intention of starting a fight in that room; a knife in the ribs or a length of piping on the head would be only too easy. There might be a chance when they got him out of the house or, more likely, while driving through the streets. He merely kept his hands behind him and waited. In a very few minutes there came the sound of a car stopping outside and the man called Ed returned. At once the two who had been sitting down got up and came to either side of Hambledon. One of them threw an old coat round his shoulders, drew it over his head, and buttoned the two top buttons so that his face was completely shrouded. An old Army greatcoat, probably; the material was rough and rasped his skin; also, it smelt of mouldy hay. They took him by the arms and led him out.

"I say, Ed"—in the tone of one having a bright idea—"your car got a luggage place behind?"

"Course it has. All them big Packards———"

"Let's put him in there, then no one'll see him if they do stop the car anywheres."

"If it isn't locked," said the voice belonging to Ed.

They came out upon the street and Hambledon felt the barrel of a gun in his ribs.

"One chirp out of you and you'll get this."

The car was drawn up so close to the house door that Hambledon had no room to move. The neck button of the coat was upon his forehead and the next below his chin; there was a narrow vertical gap between through which he could see with one eye. Ed was at the back of the car.

"It's open," he said, "but it's not big enough. We'll never shut it on him."

"Put him inside—quick! There's someone coming round the———"

44

One man leapt into the back of the car, Hambledon was hustled in after him, and another sprang in beside him. Before the door was shut the driver was in his place and the fourth man was beside him. The car moved forward, rolling and bumping on the uneven road. They slowed for the corner, turned left, and went steadily on.

Hambledon twisted in his seat and immediately two large hands closed round his neck; they were strong hands and even through the muffling folds of the coat the effect was strangling. They held the coat tightly over nose and mouth and it was impossible to breathe; Hambledon struggled violently.

"What you doing, Ackie? Keep him quiet, can't you?" The man beside the driver turned in his seat. "You're stifling him, you fool."

"Don't matter if I do——"

Hambledon got both feet on the back of the driver's seat and heaved so violently that the seat slid forward and the driver complained.

"What the hell you playing at? Suppose I can drive with you——"

"Let him breathe, Ackie!"

The strangle hold eased and Hambledon, who had got to the stage where the lungs pump vainly and the world turns black before the eyes, lay back gasping.

"You keep quiet. Next time, I won't let go."

They were passing through lighted streets. Hambledon moved his head so that, through the gap in the coat, he could get a good view of the driver, who of course was Edberg. The blond Teutonic type with nothing remarkable about him, as the police had said, and since he drove with the trained chauffeur's immobility Tommy could only get a three-quarter view of the back of the man's head and could not be sure of knowing him again. Tommy moved so as to bring his left eye to bear upon the other man in the front seat, who immediately obliged by turning round to look at him. Hambledon recognized him at once from the police photographs; that was Gruiter. Since Ackermann was on Tommy's right in the back seat,

45

the man on his left was almost certainly Claussen.

"He seems quiet enough now," said Gruiter.

"Probably fainted from fright," said Ackermann.

Hambledon kept still and said nothing, but his hands were in front of him now, hidden but ready for action.

The car slowed down and there was suddenly a shocking burst of profanity from Edberg. "They've barricaded the road."

"They're letting that car through," said Gruiter, "look. They're moving the bar. Get on his tail, Ed."

"I don't like it," said Edberg, and his voice ran up the scale.

Ackermann, in the corner beside Hambledon, sat forward suddenly.

"So you're yellow, are you?" he snarled. "Know what we do to them as turns——"

"*Ach!*" said Edberg in an exasperated voice, and swung the car round to follow the other before the barrier—merely a pole on trestles—could be replaced. The car ahead went on fast and Edberg followed it in spite of shouts from the Russian guard on the barrier. The car in front took a side turning, but Edberg went straight on.

"There you are," said Ackermann, "we're through. Nothing to get windy about."

A light came through the rear window—the headlight of something following them—then the roar of a motorcycle engine and the sound of a horn, commanding, insistent, repeated. Claussen came out of his corner and, leaning heavily on Hambledon as though he had been put there for an arm rest, looked back out of the rear window.

"Soldier on a motorcycle," he reported. "Got a sub-machine gun on the handle bars."

Edberg, who had instinctively eased a little and pulled in to let an overtaking vehicle pass, uttered a moan of terror and put his foot down hard on the accelerator. The car leapt forward; there was one more warning hoot from behind and then a burst of machine-gun fire from the following motorcycle. The back window of the car

46

was shattered, fragments of glass flew about, and Claussen uttered a surprised grunt and fell on Hambledon.

"Anybody hurt?" asked Gruiter.

"Claus," said Ackermann briefly. He turned round, rested his hand on the back of the seat, and fired several shots from Hambledon's automatic at the motorcyclist. He could hardly miss, the man was by then only ten yards behind. There was a slithering crash and then silence.

"Got him," said Ackermann in a satisfied voice.

"You blasted fool," said Gruiter furiously, "they'll have us all for this! Ed, take the next turning off wherever it goes."

Hambledon had wriggled sufficiently free of Claussen to undo his coat buttons and get ready to jump. This could not last.

Another single headlight, coming to meet them this time.

"Another soldier," wailed Edberg, "with a——"

"Down here!" snapped Gruiter.

The car braked so violently that Ackermann shot forward against Gruiter; Claussen rolled off Hambledon and back into his corner as Edberg took a corner on two wheels with a horrible crunch of a front wing against a wall. He got round only to be faced with an impassable barrier of rubble almost across the street. The car tilted sickeningly, slowed, turned, and rammed the opposite wall.

Edberg was out almost before the car stopped, over the rubble and away. Gruiter and Ackermann were almost as quick. Hambledon sprang out after them as the motorcyclist turned at the end of the street and his headlight lit up the scene. Hambledon was hardly out of the car when a figure dodged from behind and seized him by the hand.

"This way, mister——"

"Frett!"

"*Come on.*"

They ran up the slope of rubble into the ruined house from which it came and immediately slipped and rolled

47

into a large hole. A cellar, in fact, open to the sky. Frett was on his feet at once.

"Hurt, mister? Come on, run!"

Tommy picked himself up and staggered after the boy, who appeared to be able to see in the dark. They were in a passage of some kind; at the end of it Frett stopped.

"Down here. There's a hole in the floor and a ladder going down. Kneel down and feel for it. Got it? That's right. I'll go first."

Hambledon felt the edge of a square hole and, within it, the top rung of an iron ladder fixed to one side and descending vertically.

"Nothing," he said, aloud and in English, "could equal my distaste for——"

In the distance by the way they had come he heard suddenly the voice of the soldier, shouting: "Come out or I fire," or words to that effect. The threat was idle because he could not possibly see them, but it made up Hambledon's mind for him.

"Except going back to meet you," he concluded, and climbed down the ladder after Frett.

5 THE BLIND MAN

They were in a tunnel, a round tunnel such as receive and deliver underground railway trains, but not nearly so large. This one was only about five feet in diameter and Tommy walked along it with his head bent and his arms outstretched to touch the side walls. His feet sank in a couple of inches of soft mud and the smell was unseemly.

"Frett. What is this?"

"It used to be a sewer, but they don't use it now."

"I should hope not!"

"It comes out—careful, there's an opening on your left—in a yard. We'll have to mind we aren't seen there, and then it's only to cross a road and we're out of the Russian zone. I say, mister?"

"What?"

"Is this worth ten marks?"

"It's worth twenty," said Hambledon, "or it will be when we get out of this smell."

Frett laughed and plodded on.

"I say, mister?"

"Well?"

"Was any of that lot killed?"

"Claussen was. The others got away. Which reminds me, Frett, how did the shooting come to miss you? You were in the luggage boot, of course."

"They left it open when they drove off in such a tear, so I hopped on."

"Yes, but when the firing started——"

"I lay down flat. Mister, I went so flat I nearly pushed myself through the floor. Mister, you could have posted me in a letter box, honest."

Hambledon wondered whether the Russian soldier had seen the boy and mercifully aimed high; it seemed most probable, as otherwise it would be more natural to aim at the tank or the back tyres. If so, he had deserved a better fate than being shot by Ackermann.

"We're nearly there," said Frett, and Hambledon sighed with relief. A few more heavy paces and Frett stopped.

"Here's the ladder. Look up, you can see the light. I'll go first and see if there's anyone about, see, 'cause I know where to look. You come on after but not too close, I might have to dodge back."

But there was no one about and they emerged in a yard almost full of handbarrows.

"What the workers clear the roads with," explained Frett. "This way."

They came out on an unfrequented road and, since the Russians cannot possibly watch every yard of their zonal frontier, they crossed it unobserved and stepped out more freely. Frett sniffed.

"Mister," he said with awful frankness, "don't you stink!"

"You're no bunch of orchids yourself," said Hamble-

49

don indignantly. "Like to come to my hotel and have a bath, Frett?"

"What, me? They'd throw me out!"

"Oh no, they wouldn't!"

"No, mister, thank you very much. Frau Muller's got my water hot anyway; it is Saturday night. No, mister, I'd rather not, honest."

Hambledon did not insist.

"By the way, Frett, why call me 'mister' all the time? What's 'mein Herr' done that you don't like him?"

"Because you're English," said Frett simply. "That's right, isn't it? What you say in England?"

"And what d'you say to Americans?"

"Hiya, bud!"

"And when it's a Frenchman?"

"I've never met one. Look, mister—mein Herr—there's your hotel. I'll get along now."

Hambledon gave him twenty marks which Frett accepted with some dignity, for he had certainly earned them.

"And when you want me, mister, I'll be round about Sachs' place."

"Frett. Be very careful about those men. They're looking out for you. They said so. They meant to get you tonight, and only one of them is dead. Be careful tonight and meet me at Sachs' at twelve tomorrow."

"*Auf Wiedersehen*, mein Herr."

Hambledon returned to his hotel and, since there was no one about, went behind the reception desk to remove his shoes. The porter came out from the back regions somewhere and asked whether he could, perhaps, help the Herr in some way.

"I'm not drunk, if that's what you're thinking——"

"No, no, mein Herr——"

"But I appear to have trodden in something."

The porter bent forward impulsively and drew back as quickly.

"The Herr does, indeed, seem to have met with some kind of misfortune."

50

"They are good shoes," said Hambledon thoughtfully. "Normally, that is. Perhaps if they were scraped and then scrubbed and then well aired——"

He put his hand in his pocket to draw out some money and the porter took the hint.

"Leave them with me, mein Herr. They shall receive attention."

"I can go up in my socks," said Hambledon, stepping back, "if you'll take me up in the lift. Oh, Lord! My socks too!"

"And the Herr's trousers also," said the porter with lively curiosity. "The Herr would appear at some point to have taken the wrong turning."

"You may say that I was regrettably misled. About these things——"

"I will go with the Herr to his room and he shall give me such things as require attention. They shall be returned tomorrow if that is convenient."

Hambledon said that it was and led the way to the lift with long strides. He was understandably anxious not to meet any of his fellow guests. The porter waited upstairs while he removed everything he wore, except his vest which seemed to have escaped contamination, and then took away the offending garments.

"I do not wish to be called early tomorrow," said Hambledon. "I expect to spend most of the night having a series of baths.'"

The porter wished him good refreshment and left the room. The bath water was already running before he shut the door. He went down in the lift, sent off the second bootboy, protesting vainly, to the all-night cleaners, and had hardly returned to his desk when the revolving doors spun round to admit a detective-inspector of police and his sergeant.

"The Herr Hambledon is staying here, is he?"

"Certainly, gentlemen."

"Does he happen to be in?"

"Certainly he is. He came in a quarter of an hour ago and is now in his room."

51

"You are quite sure?"

"Quite sure," said the porter firmly. "I have myself only just returned from taking him up to his room."

"Taking him up. Why, is he hurt or ill? You have an automatic lift here, I think."

"The Herr was not ill," said the porter hesitantly.

"I will go up myself and see him," said the detective-inspector decidedly. "What is his number and on which floor?"

"He won't want to see you just now. He is having a bath. Several baths."

"What is all this?"

"The Herr said he must have trodden in something. I have just sent his suit, his socks, and shoes to the cleaners. I think the Herr is given to understatement."

"Like that, was it? Take me up. I must see him."

The porter shrugged his shoulders in a resigned manner and took them up. There was a sound of rushing water, Hambledon was just running in his second bath as the porter knocked at the door.

"Go away!" shouted Hambledon, but the porter said it was the police and the detective-inspector added that he was most unhappy at disturbing the Herr but that he had had definite orders to make sure that the Herr was safe and well.

"Of course I'm well. I'm having a bath. I'll come round and see you in the morning." Hambledon turned off the taps. The detective-inspector said in an apologetic voice that his orders were to see Hambledon, literally see him with his own eyes; and two or three of the other hotel guests gathered hopefully in the corridor. The porter noticed them.

"Mein Herr," he said imploringly with his mouth against the keyhole, "there is a crowd which begins to assemble. The good name of the hotel——"

"Oh, hell!" said Tommy violently. He cast a bath towel about himself and opened the door wide enough to let the detective-inspector sidle in. "What on earth is all this fuss about?"

"From information received we were led to believe that the Herr had been abducted in a car with Eastern zone number plates."

"Who told you that?"

"A message was telephoned. A most circumstantial message that you were seen to be abducted by four men, names given."

"The names were known to you?"

"Certainly, mein Herr. The men are being diligently sought for."

"Did you know the voice?"

They did not. It was a young voice, probably a boy's or even a girl's.

Hambledon remembered having warned Frett against Gruiter and his friends. If this was Frett's idea of removing the danger, there was no need to be anxious about him. He could look after himself very capably indeed.

"Yes, I see. It is all perfectly true. I was abducted by four men but, as you see, they did not manage to keep me. Persevere in your search; I hope you find them. By the way, there are only three now, Claussen is dead."

"Leaving Gruiter, Ackermann, and Edberg. Is that right? Good. Has the Herr any idea where they are now?"

"I left them in the Russian zone but I shouldn't think they'll stay there. I don't know, they might. The Russians don't know who shot the soldier."

"Shot the sol—— The Herr has had quite an evening, has he not?"

"My regards to your superintendent," said Hambledon firmly. "I will tell him all about it in the morning."

The detective-inspector took the hint.

Two days later Spelmann came to Berlin in response to a summons from Hambledon.

"As I told you," he said, "I've identified the four, but I'm not sure that we're really much further on. Look at 'em. Claussen was a jewel thief when he was alive; Christian charity forbids me to speculate upon what he has now become. I mean, the devil looks after his own, doesn't he? Edberg, ex-chauffeur, is a car thief according to the police. Gruiter is an oddly inefficient burglar——"

"So the police say," said Spelmann. "I must point out that they only know about two cases in which he was involved. In the first he was markedly unlucky, for who expects to be chased along a street by a record-breaking quarter-miler? In the second case he was certainly careless; nobody ought to walk out of a house into the arms of a policeman. Do you not think, my dear Herr Hambledon, that it may have been a long run of successes which made him careless?"

"Fingerprints at Königswinter," said Hambledon reminiscently. "Still, you may be right. Perhaps he just has his off days. Ackermann is a thug, and I would add 'pure and simple' if I were not so sure that he is neither. Spellmann, what sent that bunch of petty crooks travelling all the way to the Rhineland to steal aircraft designs?"

"Somebody sent them," said Spellmann, nodding until his white hair stood up like the crest of a cockatoo.

"If they are caught and brought in——" said Hambledon.

"We shall be no further on," finished Spelmann. "The Herr is quite right. They must be watched for and followed. I will speak to the police to that effect."

"They know me by sight," said Hambledon. "Gruiter and company, I mean."

"Yes, but they don't know me."

"They may have seen your photograph. That article in that picture paper, the *Frankfurter Illustrierte*——"

"A blunder," agreed Spelmann, "a grave blunder. Not the article, which was carefully written to give an impression of the omniscience of the police and so to alarm the criminals, but the photograph. Mein Herr, I absolutely forbade a photograph and when I saw the article I was furiously angry, but what could I do then?"

"Too late. Photographs are the devil," said Hambledon feelingly. "I have spent half my life dodging them. However, one must face the consequences. It is mainly your hair, you know. Could you not wear a hat? And use some of the fixative stuff so widely advertised?"

54

Spelmann smiled. "I thought you were going to ask me to have my hair cropped, and I do not wish to do that. You are quite right. I will attend to the matter."

Hambledon nodded. "One thing more. If these men are not to be arrested, the boy Frett should be got away. He is not safe here."

"He has brains and a quick intelligence, from what you tell me, but what can one do with a boy who will not go to school?"

"I've been talking to him and I gather that it's being a boarder he doesn't like. If he had work of some kind during the day he would attend night school. He is ambitious. After all, boarding schools are rather like nice clean prisons, aren't they?"

"Is he honest?" asked Spelmann bluntly, and Hambledon hesitated.

"He has that reputation, so Sachs the cobbler tells me, but it may be only because he has not been found out. But if I explained to him that one little theft would ruin his career for ever and ever and that he would sink back into the gutter and end in misery and crime, it might do some good."

"You talk to him again," said Spelmann. "Then, if you think he means to make good, we will find him employment in Bonn."

"I'll see him this afternoon," said Hambledon.

Later that day he passed in the street a short, sturdy figure whose walk and general outline were familiar to him but the abundant white hair was no longer in evidence. It was brushed sleekly back and covered by a blue beret drawn well down; the bright alert eyes were masked by tinted glasses with broad tortoise-shell rims. Spelmann was not unrecognizable by anyone who knew him well, but he was very unlike the photograph in the *Frankfurter Illustrierte*.

The police had received orders not to arrest three wanted men but to shadow them. A couple of days passed, and there was no sign of any of the three.

"They have gone to earth," said the chief of police, "in

55

some cellar and will stay there till they think the hunt has died down. We shall get them eventually."

"They know the police, plain-clothes branch and all," said Spelmann privately to Hambledon. "When a policeman comes into view they just vanish and appear again when he is gone. What is needed is for one of them to be seen by someone they do not recognize." He took a comb from his breast pocket, smoothed down his already sleek hair, and replaced his beret.

"Provided they have not remained in the Russian zone," said Hambledon, "voluntarily or otherwise." He occupied some of the waiting time by arranging for a friend of his to take a rather subdued Frett to Cologne and find him employment where he would be looked after. "Go with this Herr," said Hambledon. "Take the work he finds for you and stick to it. Go to evening classes and get yourself educated. Learn languages. Behave yourself and keep out of mischief. I will come and see you when I leave here. Don't let me down. Good-bye."

In the end it was Spelmann who was the first to see one of the men, and it was Gruiter, the most easily recognized because of the police photographs and description. Spelmann was wandering vaguely along; there are so many who wander vaguely in a city where a quarter of the working population are unemployed. It was towards evening, at the time when twilight is falling but the lamps are not yet lighted in the streets. Gruiter came out of an alley, looked cautiously about him, and went on ahead of Spelmann, who followed unconcernedly after him. Gruiter turned into a small shop which sold picture post cards, newspapers, writing materials, and a few cheap novels, and the door shut behind him.

Spelmann waited. He was prepared to wait for hours if necessary, but in less than ten minutes the door opened again and a woman, whom he correctly assumed to be the shopkeeper, came out helping a blind man down the three steep steps to the pavement. The blind man thanked her; she returned to the shop, and he set off slowly along

56

the street, tapping the pavement edge with his white stick.

"Almost he fooled me," said Spelmann to Hambledon, later that evening. "He was wearing a hat instead of a cap, very dark glasses, and an overcoat, but he had not changed his trousers or his boots. So I followed. It was easy, as he went slowly. Also, I think his glasses—they looked almost black—really did make it hard for him to see plainly, for at one crossing he stepped in front of a car and was nearly run over. Someone dragged him back and a kind policeman helped him across the road."

Hambledon laughed.

"I did not notice the policeman's number," said Spelmann. "My own district is very far away and I have some tact. Gruiter went on till he reached a café, one of those places with tables outside, not actually on the pavement but only divided from it by a railing. A terrace, perhaps; it was one step higher than the pavement. There was a girl sitting at a table against the railing; when she saw Gruiter coming she ran out and led him in, back to her table. I also felt that it would be pleasant to sit, but I could not get very near them so I sat where I could see them, if I could not hear. I also was against the railings. There was another man watching them from across the road, he was there when Gruiter and I arrived, so he was presumably watching the girl."

"Just a moment," said Hambledon. "I gather the café terrace was fairly full, how then did you know which of the assembled company he was watching?"

"Because of what followed later, mein Herr."

"I beg your pardon. Tell me about him."

"I shall know him again. A thin young man who coughed frequently and bent forwards when he did so. One would say that the cough hurt him. He was neatly and warmly dressed, but he was hollow-chested and his shoulders came forward. His face also was thin, the bones showed under the skin; he had high cheekbones and a heavy frontal bar above his eyes like the busts of Beethoven. You know what I mean?"

"Perfectly. I should almost recognize him myself."

"Good. It may be useful."

Spelmann said that Gruiter, as a blind man, acted very well. The girl helped him with his coffee, putting it within easy reach and guiding his fingers to the cup; when he was talking to her he did not always look straight towards her but sometimes over one or other of her shoulders. He was very careful how he moved. One would say that he had not been blind long.

"Those dark glasses," suggested Hambledon.

"Exactly, mein Herr. He had only suffered from this affliction—what—perhaps twenty minutes." They were talking earnestly together; as they did so the girl rested her elbow upon the top of the rail and leaned her cheek upon her hand. "She was wearing a ring, mein Herr, and what a ring! It was large and heavy; she wore it upon her middle finger. There was an elaborate setting, and one large diamond. Such a diamond! It was like a car head lamp."

"Really, Spelmann! A duchess in disguise?"

"I may, perhaps, exaggerate a little," admitted Spelmann. "I cannot imagine a duchess being of the type which this girl represented, but perhaps I have an old-fashioned respect for rank. I call her a girl, but she was not very young and I have seldom seen such a hard face. I looked at her and said to myself that if she had a pet name it ought to be *Tigerin*."

"You don't seem to have been attracted."

"Presently an old man came wandering along the pavement; very old, very feeble, very bent. An animated rag bag and not very animated. One would say the spark of life burned low in him."

"Oh, get on, Spelmann!"

"At the moment when he came level with her table she had her hand resting on the rail and the ring came, so to speak, under his eyes. He stopped and stared at it closely; she noticed it and took her hand away. He put his arm over the rail, took hold of her wrist, and pulled her hand up to look again at the ring. She shook him

58

off and spoke roughly to him, but all he did was to go back to the entrance, into the terrace, and along to her table. He passed near me, mein Herr; he was muttering to himself, I could not understand what he said because he was not speaking German."

"What was it?"

"Russian or Polish. I can hardly tell them apart. He was animated enough then. One would have thought the ring some magic talisman to give him new life. He reached their table and addressed them in German. Simple German, such as one speaks who has learned it late in life. 'That ring. It is not yours. It is stolen. You have stolen it.'"

"Probably quite true."

"So I thought. The woman denied it, covering the ring with her other hand, and Gruiter stood up and said the old man was drunk. He poked at the old man with his white stick, saying: 'Go away! You are drunk. You annoy the lady,' poking at him all the time. People were turning round and standing up to look. I also. Suddenly the old man collapsed into the chair Gruiter had been sitting on and laid his head on the table, and, at that, the woman seized Gruiter by the hand and pulled him away. She threw down a note on the table so nobody tried to stop them and they hurried away. It was at this point that I was sure the young man across the road was interested in them and none other, for the moment they began to make their way out he straightened up; when they came out upon the pavement he moved forward; and when they walked quickly away he hurried also, crossing the road to keep behind them. I also would have followed but that they were nearer the exit than I, and you know what it is trying to get out of a café when the tables and chairs are all disarranged. I had not gone far before a waiter arrived and spoke to the old man. He was not unkind. He said: 'Mein Herr, get up. It is not allowed, to sleep here,' and he pulled him back. Then the old man fell sideways over the arm of the chair like a doll of which the sawdust has run out."

"Was he dead?" asked Hambledon.

"I did not like the look of him," said Spelmann, who was never to be diverted from his own way of telling a story. "I thought he had had a heart attack, but when he was withdrawn from the table there was a red stain upon the cloth and it was not a wine stain, mein Herr."

"Not even 'Dragon's Blood'? Had he been stabbed?"

"Shot. I went across to him and he was not dead. The police came and then an ambulance and he was taken to hospital."

"Shot. Did you hear it?"

"No. That is, there was a good deal of noise and all the time there had been corks popping occasionally. I did not hear anything of which I could say to myself: 'Heinrich, that was a shot.' "

"Do you know which hospital they took him to?"

"Yes," said Spelmann, and named it.

"Come on," said Hambledon.

When they reached the hospital they interviewed the surgeon whose patient the old man was.

"To be frank with you," said the surgeon, "I don't think a lot of his chances, though the bullet wound is not really serious. It went through his side and out again, chipping one rib but not penetrating the lung. If he were a younger man he would be out again in a week, but he is very old and very tired, also he has been half starved for some time. He is wandering in his mind and he talks to himself or, perhaps, to people who are not there."

"What does he say?" asked Hambledon eagerly.

"Can you speak Polish? I can't."

"Oh, dear. I suppose he hasn't got any papers?"

"Oh yes, he has. All present and correct. His name is Karas. Apparently he has drifted here from Poland. He is illiterate and was here for some time before he learned that there was a refugee organization he could apply to

60

for help. The police told me all this. He has been before the Committee and was to have gone again tomorrow. They think he will get official recognition but whether they'll get him out of Berlin is more doubtful. These refugees have to be flown out, you know, and there are many citizens more useful than poor old Karas awaiting transport. Still, he'll be looked after."

"May we see him?"

"You can go and look at him, certainly; I'll take you along myself. There is another case in that ward I want to have a look at before I pack up for the night. But you won't be able to talk to him, he'll have had a sedative and I hope he's asleep. Whether he is or not, I won't have him disturbed."

"Did he," asked Spelmann, "have anything else in his pockets besides his official identity papers which, I suppose, the Refugee Committee gave him?"

"I'm sure I don't know," said the surgeon. "If he had, they'll be in his locker. The ward Sister will know, or ought to."

They stood beside the narrow bed in which the old man lay; his hair, his face, and the grey blankets were only slightly different tones of the same colour. He was deeply asleep, his mouth a little open and the wrinkled eyelids sunken over his eyes.

"Poor old man," said the young nurse who had been bidden to escort Hambledon and Spelmann. "He'll look better tomorrow when he's had a shave."

"You think he'll get over it?"

The nurse lifted her shoulders. "He's had a shock, of course, and he's very frail, but it's wonderful how tough some old people are. He's got every chance here."

"I'm sure of that," said Hambledon. "The Herr Chirurg Weissmuller said that we might see whatever he had in his pockets."

"Precious little," said the nurse. "A few photographs. No letters, no money, no tobacco." She unlocked the bedside cupboard and gave them what had once been an expensive crocodile-leather wallet, now in the last stages of decrepitude and held together by a piece of string. Hambledon opened it to find some half-dozen photographs mounted on card, professional photographs rubbed and faded with age but still clear. There was an immensely imposing figure of a man in an elaborate uniform covered with orders. He stood stiffly against a pillar and his hand was on his sword. Another showed a lady in full evening dress with necklace, tiara, bracelets, and rings on her fingers. She sat with great dignity in a stiff armchair but her face was kind. Across the back of this was written: "Mikhail. Christmas 1921," in a pointed, educated hand.

"That was never him?" said Spellmann in an awestruck voice, referring to the personage by the pillar.

"Oh no," said Hambledon, "he's illiterate, don't you remember? These are Master and Mistress, I expect. Is his name Mikhail? Let's look—yes, that's right. Mikhail Karas. Here's the family castle, no doubt. Gosh, it's as big as Ehrenbreitstein and much older. Much. Here's a group of the staff all seemly disposed on the grand staircase in order of seniority; scullions on the extreme left, under-housemaids on the extreme right, and who's this in the middle?" Hambledon took a small magnifying glass from his pocket. "Yes, here we are, I'd take a bet on it. Poor old Mikhail Karas, in person, dressed up in a tail coat all over gold lace and dignity. The butler, I fancy. Look for yourself."

Spelmann looked and nodded, ran his eyes along the orderly ranks of servants, and uttered a subdued exclamation.

"What is it?"

"That man there—a footman, is he?—he's the young man with the cough who followed Gruiter and the woman this evening."

Hambledon took the photograph back.

"Yes, I see. Just as you described him. Not a face which would alter much from the cradle to the grave. This is damned odd. They must have known each other in the old days. I wonder whether——"

He stopped, for Spelmann was showing him a photograph he had not yet seen. It was of the young footman alone in the glory of a creaseless livery with a self-conscious smirk upon his face. Across the corner was written: "Your loving son."

"His son," said Hambledon. "His son? Yet, when the poor old boy is struck down, the young Karas doesn't even cross the road to see if he's ill?" He looked down at the sleeping man. "What a damned rotten—I suppose he saw what happened?"

"He might not have done," said Spelmann. "Gruiter was standing up and so was the woman; they would mask this man from view. Also, there were passers-by and traffic. Then, when they went away, this poor man only looked as though he were sitting down; unhappy, perhaps, but not obviously hurt. No, if young Karas' errand were urgent enough, I doubt if he would think it necessary to abandon it."

"No, perhaps not. I may be doing him an injustice. But, when he hears what has happened, will he not come here, Spelmann?"

"We will make the necessary arrangements," said Spelmann. "There is one more photograph, is there not?"

"Only a small boy on a pony. The son of the house?"

"Any name on the back?"

Hambledon deciphered the inscription with difficulty, for the ink was faded and the lights in the ward were dimmed for the night.

"Paul Alexis Rudolph Patro—no, Pastolsky, aged ten. Quite a—— What's the matter?" For Spelmann had uttered a wordless grunt and stood staring with his mouth open as though he had seen a ghost.

"Pastolsky—you are sure it is Pastolsky?"

Hambledon went nearer a light and spelt it out carefully. "Yes, that's right. Why?"

"Did I not tell you—— No, evidently not. Pastolsky was the name of General Knipe's Polish cousins."

"Didn't know he had any!"

"Oh, yes. His mother was a Pastolsky and he could speak Polish, naturally. That is why he was employed in

63

Poland; and I daresay he made an opportunity of protecting his cousins as far as he could."

Hambledon put the photographs back in the wallet, tied it up again, and looked round for the young nurse who had tactfully retired to a distance. She came up, smiling, and Hambledon gave her the packet to lock up again.

"I know you'd take great care of him, whoever he was. But he is a good old man, I believe. He once held a position of great trust and he treasures the souvenirs of it. It is sad to see him lying like this, in a casual ward."

"Poor old boy," she said. "We'll do all we can, be sure of that. Will you be coming again?"

"Oh yes," said Hambledon, "and I hope you'll be on duty when we do."

She laughed softly and motioned them away. Hambledon took Spelmann by the arm and led him out of the ward with long strides, down the stairs, and out into the street. Spelmann began to say something but Hambledon hushed him imperatively. "Just a moment, if you don't mind. I'm trying to work it out."

They hurried through the streets to Hambledon's hotel; dinner was long over but they were served with sandwiches and beer in a quiet corner of the deserted dining room. As soon as the waiter had gone out of earshot Hambledon, with a sandwich in one hand and a pint pot in the other, leaned across the table.

"Listen, Spelmann. Let me retell the story as far as we know or can guess. Stop me if I go wrong. Renzow lives at Königswinter; he is an aircraft designer. General Knipe is—was—his brother-in-law. General Knipe's mother was a Pastolsky. The Pastolskys live in Poland in a castle and in a style suitable to royalty. We have seen tonight a photograph showing some of their jewels. All right so far? Good. General Knipe was in Poland towards the end of the war, until the Army he commanded fell back upon Berlin before the advancing Russians. Sometime when they first arrived in Berlin, Knipe gets leave and goes to Renzow at Königswinter, where the first thing he does is to go to Bonn and buy a hulking great safe which he has installed in Renzow's house. Now tell me what was kept in Renzow's safe."

"The Pastolsky jewels."

"Or some of them. Edberg was General Knipe's batman-chauffeur. If he drove the car when Knipe went on leave, or even before—or both—he must at the very least have known that something precious was being carried. It would not be left unguarded for a moment, for example. Besides, I expect he helped to carry them in, and no doubt the Pastolsky jewels were well known. No, on second thoughts, he wasn't perfectly sure that the boxes or what-have-you contained jewels; that was why Claussen was invited to join the party. He could give them the once-over. Well?"

"Go on," said Spelmann, nodding his head like a mandarin. "Go on."

"One step at a time. There were no jewels in the safe when we saw it——"

"And there was something Anna Knipe was not willing to tell me. I said so at the time," said Spelmann.

"You did. So those four scoundrels got away with the jewels. What did they do with them?"

"Bring them to Berlin?" said Spelmann in a doubtful voice. "Through the Russian controls on the Berlin highway?"

"I wouldn't," said Hambledon, "would you? But they brought some of them along to go on with, for I think you saw one of them tonight."

"The ring that wretched harpy of a woman was wearing," said Spelmann. *"Du lieber Gott,* if they are all like that the whole collection is worth a king's ransom. This, of course, is where the Karas men come into it."

"Yes. I suppose Karas junior recognized it on her finger and followed her to that café. Then Karas senior comes mooning along and also sees it and recognizes it and makes a fuss, and rightly in my opinion. No wonder young Karas was so taken up with the woman that he didn't notice poor Father sitting down with a bump in the chair. Even if he did, he may have thought that Father could wait; probably they live somewhere near that café since they were both in that street, though not together. When he gets home and finds Father hasn't——" Hambledon's voice died away.

"You mean, *if* he gets home. Gruiter and that awful woman——"

"And Edberg and Ackermann. Especially Ackermann," said Hambledon thoughtfully.

"By the way," said Spelmann, "we never left word at the hospital to let us know if young Karas came to see his father. That was what I was about to say when we were leaving."

"And I shut you up. I'm sorry. In the excitement of the moment I forgot all about it and I wouldn't have gone back then, anyway. We can ring them up in the morning, first thing. It will do just as well. If he doesn't come——"

"We shall, at least, know who is responsible."

Hambledon shrugged his shoulders. "Don't you think," he said in a lighter tone, "that your tigress woman was a great fool to wear a ring like that so openly? There are plenty of people in Berlin, or anywhere else, who'd cut her throat for a tenth of its value by your description."

"She may not have believed it to be real. I myself wondered. That showy stuff which looks so opulent, what do they call it? Costume jewellery, is it not? Too big to be true. Or perhaps she had not had it long and could not forbear to wear it. Who knows? They say women are like that."

The two bachelors shook their heads solemnly over the vagaries of women and sent their pint pots to be refilled.

"And now, Spelmann, what becomes of your aircraft designs?"

"I expect they were duds, after all," said Spelmann sorrowfully. "She said so. Anna Knipe, I mean."

"I think it will be necessary to try to make sure. Perhaps she will talk now we know what she was hiding up. Or Renzow may recover consciousness."

"He had not, when I came away. Where are the jewels, mein Herr?"

"You tell me," urged Hambledon.

But when Hambledon rang up the hospital as early in the morning as he thought seemly, he was told that Mikhail Karas had died in his sleep during the night.

"Oh dear. Oh, I'm sorry to hear that. By the way, I hate bothering you, but if any of his relatives come to see him I particularly want to speak to them. I believe he has a son in Berlin and I—what? Already been? Just gone. How very unfortunate."

The ward Sister explained that a young man came to enquire about Mikhail Karas. Asked if he were any relative, the young man said that he was the old man's son. Asked to prove it, he said there was a photograph of himself in his father's wallet. The likeness was so unmistakable that he was instantly believed, and the sad news was broken to him. He saw the body in the mortuary, said again that that was his father, and made arrangements for the funeral. He then went away, taking the wallet with him. No, not long ago; about half an hour perhaps. No, he had left no address.

"So we've missed him," said Hambledon to Spelmann.

"Yes. But we have now a number of people to look for; all of whom we shall recognize if we see them, and any one of whom will give us a lead to the others. Gruiter, Edberg, Ackermann, the tigress woman, and young Karas, who probably knows where to lay his hands on them after following them yesterday."

"Laying his hands on them is probably what he is trying to do," said Hambledon grimly, "and not in the way of kindness, either."

"My money's on the others," said Spelmann with a sigh. "Four to one, and the one a consumptive if I am not mistaken."

"Perhaps he'll attend the funeral," said Hambledon hopefully. "We will do so ourselves."

They did, but only two or three poor neighbours followed the coffin through a depressing downpour of rain. One of them was the old woman whose lodger Mikhail

Karas had been; Hambledon spoke to her after the service.

"He was a good old man who had seen better days," she said. "He was considerate and gave no trouble. He used to tell me long stories about the great castle and his master's family. He said they were all dead, mein Herr; and that it was time that he died too and went to serve them in heaven." She wiped her eyes. "He was very simple in heart; he would have been proud to think that a *gnadig* Herr such as yourself should have followed him to the grave."

"But his son," said Hambledon, "did he not live with him?"

"Oh no, mein Herr. The son does not live in Berlin. I do not know where he lives. Somewhere far away. He came to see my poor old lodger two or three times this last week, but he was not lodging with us. He is in bad health, mein Herr. He is a comsumptive. He was in a concentration camp where he almost died, but some kind German friends got him out. His father told me about it many times—how his son would have died if it had not been for his good friends. The young man paid for the funeral, of course—the undertaker's men told me so—and I expected to see him here. I do not know why he is not here. One would naturally expect it."

"Naturally," agreed Hambledon. "Do you know where the son is staying in Berlin?"

"No, mein Herr. They spoke much together, but in Polish, which I do not understand. He came to see his father early in the morning of the day after he had been taken to hospital, and I told the young man what had happened and where his father was. He rushed away and I have not seen or heard of him since, if it please the Herr."

It did not please the Herr at all, but there was nothing he could do but take her address and ask her to let him know if young Karas should come back. "Here is my card and the address of my hotel," said Hambledon. "If he should return, implore him to come and see me. I want to help him and I believe I can."

But Karas never returned to his father's lodgings or

appeared anywhere else. The woman with the ring was seen no more; and as for Gruiter, Ackermann, and Edberg, they might never have existed.

"If she's gone into the Russian sector we may never find her," said Hambledon. "But she may have met with some accident——"

"Or with Karas, with the same result," said Spelmann.

"At least Karas is not in any hospital here, or we should have been told."

"He may be at the bottom of a well."

"I'm not going round Berlin dragging wells," said Hambledon irritably, "but I don't mind visiting a few hospitals. You'll have to come too. You can recognize her."

"No one seems to know her in Berlin," objected Spelmann. "It is true that her description would fit several hundred women, but a woman of that sort is usually known in her district, and besides, there is the ring."

"You don't suppose she has still got it, do you?"

"Why not, if she has gone back to wherever she came from?"

"I know, now, why Job was so justly renowned for his patience! It wasn't on account of his sufferings but for the way he put up with his friends. You are Eliphaz, Bildad, and Zophar all rolled into one. Come on, exercise is good for you."

They went to see Weissmuller again, the surgeon who had treated Mikhail Karas, and told him that they were looking for a woman whose name, address, and detailed description were unknown.

"You don't know much, do you?" said the amused surgeon.

"Only that she's a shocking bad lot and the associate of criminals."

"Such women usually end up in a hospital ward," agreed the surgeon. "If she isn't in one yet she probably will be one of these days. Look, I'll ring up the ward Sister in the women's ward here and she'll let you walk round. If you don't find your woman, come back here in not more than twenty minutes, for I can't wait for you."

She was not there, and they returned to the surgeon's room to find him putting on his overcoat.

"Just in time. I am now going to a hospital for women only, staffed by nuns. You can follow me round the wards, but for God's sake keep your mouths shut. You'll see why, in a minute."

They were whirled away in the surgeon's car to another hospital, a tall, patched-up building behind a high wall. Weissmuller pulled up the car with a jerk, sending the gravel flying, and leapt out of the car with Hambledon and Spelmann hurrying after.

"This is a place where unattached males are definitely not allowed. Even attached ones are only admitted on sufferance, and subject to the most stringent precautions. Don't ask me why. I'm only a poor innocent sawbones." He led the way in at a side door and ran up a flight of stone stairs into a small room, shutting the door behind them. "You two will put on white coats and follow me round, looking as intelligent as possible but not uttering a word, for if you give me away there'll be hell to pay. Here are your coats. Put them on."

They did so while the surgeon sat at his desk and ran rapidly through a series of reports. Hambledon did not look much like a doctor, but what does a doctor look like? Spelmann was much more convincing in the part. There was a stethoscope on a shelf and he asked if he could borrow it.

"What, that? Oh, yes. It's waiting to be sent away to be repaired, anyway; I don't suppose you'll damage it much more."

Spelmann arranged it carefully in the breast pocket of his white coat after the official manner. They started with the accident ward; the surgeon said that that was his usual practice and they'd better stick to it. Weissmuller looked hard at them at the last moment and said: "Unmoved expressions, please, gentlemen. Kindly and alert, but unmoved." He walked in and they followed meekly after.

The first three or four cases they saw—and they had to

70

look attentively—proved the warning necessary. Hambledon found a remedy and whispered it to Spelmann, who was turning delicately green.

"Throw your eyes out of focus, then you won't see much. And don't scowl!"

Even so, towards the end of the ward they both turned away from one bed and engaged in a whispered consultation a couple of yards away. Spelmann's eyes wandered over the half-dozen beds remaining and stopped at the one in the corner.

"That's her," he said. "Look, Hambledon, that's the one."

7 AIR-GUN

Hambledon waited until Weissmuller turned away from the case with which he had been dealing and then went up to him and spoke in an undertone. "We've found her. The last bed on the left."

"Assault case," murmured the surgeon. "I wondered, before I brought you here. Just a moment. We'll take the ward Sister into her office and explain matters. Sister Francisca!"

Once inside the Sister's little room, one wall of which was of glass so that she could see into the ward at all times, Weissmuller laid the matter open. "I have been guilty, Sister, of a small deception. These gentlemen are not students of surgery, they are high officers of Criminal Investigation."

A gleam of humour lit up the Sister's calm face. "Your little deception was not entirely successful, Herr Chirurg. I recognized the defective stethoscope."

"You are very good, Sister——"

"I was sure that your motive was above reproach."

"Thank you," said Weissmuller. "I was anxious to avoid any excitement or talk; if these gentlemen had not found the woman they sought they would have gone quietly away and no comment would have been caused. It is the assault case in the end bed. Look, you won't want me, I'll get on with my round." He went away and they saw him pass along the ward.

"What is her name, please, madame?" asked Hambledon.

"Have you come to arrest her?"

"Oh, no. Unless she has done something of which the police are ignorant. No, I want her to tell me something, that is all. If I may talk to her privately for a little while, that is all I want."

"May I ask if the case is really serious?"

"It is murder and she knows the man who did it."

The Sister bent her head, crossed herself, and immediately became brisk and businesslike. She took a loose-leaf file from a shelf and turned over the pages.

"This is she. Do you wish to take notes? Here is a pad if you care to use it. Theresa Zingel, aged thirty-four. She was brought in here late on Tuesday night, the day before yesterday, by the police. She was found lying unconscious in the road. She had a dislocated elbow and two broken ribs, concussion of the brain, and extensive bruising generally distributed over the body. There is also some injury to the spine which may be serious."

Spelmann whistled under his breath and Hambledon said: "Badly beaten up. Was she wearing a ring when she was brought here?"

"No. Some trumpery earrings, but no ring."

"Can she talk?" asked Spelmann.

"Oh, yes. That is, she can speak without the least difficulty, but she will not give any account of herself or of her assailant. She would not even give her name or address but the police found the room in which she lived, and they brought her identity papers here. I understand ———" The Sister checked herself and became silent.

"I can get that information from the police, madame," said Hambledon quickly, and she thanked him. "Now, if we might talk to her—it is not very private here———"

"I will have screens put round the bed; it is surprising

72

how they muffle sound," said the Sister. "If you speak quietly you will not be overheard."

Five minutes later Hambledon and Spelmann were sitting on either side of the high bed and Theresa Zingel looked from one to the other with open defiance. She moved her head and her arms easily enough, but there was a complete immobility about the lower half of her body which should have aroused sympathy but did not.

"Your name," began Hambledon, "is Theresa Zingel."

"Clever, aren't you?"

"Not particularly," said Hambledon, "but I know quite a lot."

"Then you don't need me to tell you."

"Where's your ring?"

"If you could tell me that," she said, "you might be more useful than you look."

"I know where it came from," said Hambledon. "Originally, I mean. Which of them gave it to you, was it Gruiter?"

She gave him a long hard stare and then said: "No."

"Or Karl Edberg? I don't think it was Ackermann, somehow. Ackie, you call him, don't you? I don't see Anders Claussen parting with a stone like that, he knows its value too well. Knows, I said, it should have been 'knew.' He's dead, you know, the Russians shot him."

"Who the devil are you?"

"Did you know Claussen was dead?"

After a pause she said: "Yes. Gruiter told me."

"In the café when he was playing at being blind?"

That struck right home; she gasped and lay back, pushing against the pillow as though she were trying to retire through it.

"Are you police?"

"No. Who beat you up?"

"I don't know his name. He said he was the old man's son, but I don't know."

"The consumptive," said Hambledon. "Where is he?"

She smiled, a slow secretive smile. "The regions beyond the grave are an insoluble mystery to mortal man. I

73

heard that in a sermon once; it was the only bit of sense in the whole silly rigmarole."

Hambledon nodded. "All the same, what one hears at funerals seems to stick, doesn't it?"

The defiance vanished and was replaced by naked fear. "How did you know——"

"Never mind. What did you tell the old man's son?"

"He wanted to know where the jewels were. I didn't know and he wouldn't believe me. I didn't know, I still don't. He took my ring and beat me. I fought him but he went on and on, but it wasn't the pain, it was when he said he'd tell about Belsen that I gave in. You know. Where they preached that sermon over the graves afterwards, and me standing there looking mournful with a handkerchief to my eyes. Were you there too? You must have been. Were you?"

"What did you tell him?"

"I gave him their address, where they lived. I wish I'd thought of it before, it 'ud have saved all this. Then I hit him in the throat and he began to cough, so I dodged him and ran out. I meant to telephone to them but I don't think I did. I can't remember any more, only being here with all them Holy Annies creeping about."

"What was the address?"

"I'm not telling you. You'll take the police there."

"What was the address?"

"I've forgotten."

"Oh, don't be silly," said Hambledon sharply. "I can talk, can't I, just as well as the old man's son?"

She collapsed at once. "I can't stand it," she whimpered, "being tried and standing up in front of everybody and people coming to swear lies about what I did. I had to do it, didn't I? You can't pick and choose——"

"What was the address?"

Strictly speaking, it was not an address in the ordinary sense, but detailed directions for finding one semi-basement room among ruins in a city largely composed of ruins with basement rooms under them. Spelmann made notes.

"And if I don't find it," said Hambledon, preparing to go, "you know what will happen to you, don't you?"

"They'll hang me and I can't run away—— Don't, don't. Why are you so cruel?"

"Cruel!" said Hambledon, and laughed. "That's good, from you. Come on, Spelmann."

They walked back through the ward; Weismuller had gone about his business but Sister Francisca was in her glass-walled office. Hambledon stopped and she came to the door.

"I only wished to thank you, madame."

"It is I who should thank you for your careful tact in coming dressed as you are. It was thoughtful and kind."

"Don't thank me," said Hambledon hastily. "I should not have thought of it; it was the Herr Chirurg Weissmuller who did that. I—that is—that woman——"

The Sister's tranquil look remained unaltered.

"That woman," Hambledon blundered on, "do you know anything about her? She ought not——"

The Sister's uplifted hand stopped him. "Please do not tell me, mein Herr. This is a place to which the sick come to be healed in body and that is the extent of my duty. Further than that I do not wish to know."

"You are wise as well as good, madame. Let me first offer one suggestion—do not let her talk to your young nuns. If she became confidential they might hear what would come between them and their prayers for the rest of their lives."

"Thank you," she said. "I will be careful. Though, do you think I have worked in this hospital for thirty years without learning to recognize evil when I see it?"

Hambledon and Spelmann bowed to her and went out, leaving their white coats in Weissmuller's room on their way.

"And the next step?" asked Spelmann. "You will not visit these three men unsupported?"

"Listen," said Hambledon patiently. "Do I remind you of Siegfried or St. George or even Douglas Fairbanks? Or do you take me for 'the portrait of a blinking idiot'? We

75

will take with us an ample supply of large policemen. We are even now making for the head police station."

"Splendid," said Spelmann, and stepped out more confidently.

The entrance was down a flight of stone steps into a narrow area of a kind common in towns to provide light to basement rooms and a means of access to a trades-man's entrance. There even remained some part of the railings which had once fenced off the unwary or unstable passer-by from an eight-foot drop. There was a door at the foot of the steps and a window beside it—the window was closely curtained.

Hambledon, Spelmann, a police sergeant, and three constables circled round the place and came to the back. Here they found a slope leading down to a back window, but no door; there were one or two rough steps cut in the slope.

"Emergency exit only," murmured Hambledon. The po-lice sergeant gave a quiet order to two of his constables who slithered down the slope and took up their positions on either side of the window while the rest of the party returned to the front.

"Let us enquire," said Hambledon, "whether•there is anyone at home." He moved toward the head of the steps but the police sergeant, politely begging to be excused the apparent rudeness, slipped in front of him and ran down the steps with his constable at his heels. They did not knock at the door, they turned the handle; the door opened and they went straight in, revolver in hand. There was a few moments' pause and then the police sergeant reappeared in the doorway and looked up at Hambledon and Spelmann on the steps.

"Nobody at home?" said Hambledon.

The police sergeant gulped, steadied his voice, and said, yes, in a sense, there was someone there. Hamble-don pushed past him and entered the room with Spel-mann close behind; as he did so the constable pulled back the curtain from the window and let a flood of day-light into the room. When he had done this he sidled out of the room, keeping his face to the wall as he did so, and distressed noises were heard from the passage outside.

There was a wooden armchair in the room and there was a man sitting in it. He could not fall out of the chair although he was quite dead, because he had been bound to it; his arms along the arms of the chair, his legs separately to the front chair legs, and there were, in addition, cords round his chest and the back of the chair. He had been comprehensively and disgustingly tortured.

"Young Karas?" said Hambledon, and stooped to look into the man's face, for his head hung forward. "No. Not Karas. Who is this poor devil?"

The police sergeant heard the question as he came into the room with a wooden face and a complete lack of expression. He also stooped over the body and said he was not sure but it might be Edberg. "One of my men knows him personally. I'll get him in."

Hambledon dragged down the window curtain to cover the body, leaving only the face exposed. One of the constables on duty at the back came in and identified the body as that of Karl Edberg.

"Quite sure?"

"No doubt at all, sir. I knew him well."

"Do you want him left here, sir?" asked the sergeant.

"Heavens, no," said Hambledon with a shudder. "Take it away and bury it. Oh, ask the police surgeon how long he's been dead. Put it outside somewhere, chair and all. I want to examine this room."

The chair and its occupant moved crabwise out of the room with a slow tread of heavy feet while Hambledon went to the window; failing to open it he took his automatic—a replacement of the one Ackermann took from him—from his pocket; smashed the glass out with the butt and drew long breaths of fresh air.

"Ah, that's better. Well, Spelmann?"

"He was worked on to make him talk, obviously."

"Obviously. And I should think he did talk before he died. If young Karas did that, he must have learned

77

something in his concentration camp. Belsen, I suppose, since you notice he knew the Zingel woman's fatal secret."

"I suppose so. And what he wanted to know," said Spelmann, "was where the rest of the jewels are."

"Of course it was. He was avenging his father too, no doubt, but plain death would have done for that. This wasn't Gruiter, but as near as no matter. This case gets more like the ten little nigger boys with every passing day, doesn't it?"

"Indeed? I have not read the paper today."

"Read the paper?" said Hambledon, staring.

"Were you not referring to some item of news about ten Negro youths?"

"Oh, let it ride," said Tommy.

The room was poorly and scantily furnished with a truckle bed along one wall, a table under the window with a round mirror hanging above it and hairbrushes and shaving kit upon it, a small oilstove and a kettle, and three wooden chairs.

"Edberg's home, I think," said Tommy. "We have here the remains of the habit of personal smartness. He even owned a clothesbrush."

"There is a cupboard in the wall here," said Spelmann, moving towards it.

"Look out something nasty doesn't pop out and say boo."

"Nothing which merely popped and booed could be half so nasty as what we've already seen." Spelmann unlocked the door and opened it, there was a slithering sound and something did fall out on the floor. Spelmann picked it up.

"Gruiter's white stick. Here, I think, is the overcoat he was wearing. I wonder whether the dark glasses——Yes, here they are in the pocket."

The cupboard was a tall, shallow one filling one side of the chimney breast; there were other garments hanging upon hooks besides Gruiter's blind-man overcoat, and they were neatly brushed and, where necessary, mended. There was a suitcase standing upright at the bottom and

Spelmann passed it over to Hambledon, who opened it.

"Edberg's clothespress, this. Shirts, vest, socks," he said, lifting the things out one at a time and examining them singly. "By the way—I meant to ask you before—I suppose the woman who kept the little newspaper shop was questioned? The kind lady who helped the blind man down the steps."

"Oh, yes. She said a blind man did come in there sometimes and that she always helped him down the steps. She asked if it was a crime to help a blind man down steps. She didn't know who he was or anything about him, so she said. She was a hard-working shopkeeper, not a warty-nosed cop. Charged with allowing him to assume a disguise on her premises, she denied it indignantly and, since there was a back door leading to a yard with other houses behind, we could not prove that he had not simply walked through and come back. Mein Herr, there is something a little funny about this walking stick. It seems to be screwed together in sections and there is a small knob here in front of the handle which does not appear to serve——"

Hambledon spun round. Spelmann was holding the stick horizontally to examine the knob. He pressed it just as Tommy struck the stick up; there was a hard "plop" which sounded loud in that quiet room, and an air-gun slug sang over Hambledon's head and broke the last remaining pane in the window.

"Herr Gott!" gasped Spelmann, turning perfectly white. "I nearly shot you. *Gütig Himmel,* what a devil's contrivance—— *Gnadig* Herr, I shall never——"

"Cheer up," said Hambledon, taking the stick from his unresisting fingers, "there's no harm done. Even the window is not much worse than it was and at least we know now how poor old Karas was shot."

"Oh," said Spelmann, dropping into a chair to wipe his agitated forehead, "if a merciful Providence had not prompted you to turn round just now——"

"It wasn't a merciful Providence," said Hambledon. "At least, Providence may have reminded me, but when you

79

talked about screwed sections and a knob, I suddenly remembered a jumble sale in the vicarage garden when I was a lad. Somebody sent in a stick like this and there was a pumplike attachment with it. I found out how it worked and tried it out and potted the gardener, I remember. My father took reprisals. There ought to be a pump here somewhere——"

"On the floor in the cupboard," said Spelmann, diving for it like a terrier. "A brass one, very neat."

"That's it," said Hambledon. He made to unscrew the stick for a demonstration and then changed his mind. "I'll try this tonight, from my bedroom window, on the rats. In the meantime, I thought I felt something in these socks just as you——"

He unrolled a pair of socks and there slid out upon the table a gold chain bracelet with a diamond in every link.

8 FIVE RABBITS LOOSE

Spelmann replaced his beret with a regrettable cloth cap, and his shabby raincoat with a shabbier overcoat, and prowled the streets of Berlin looking for Ackermann and Gruiter. He learned to know the city as few men know it except the police. He made a number of disreputable but interesting friends and acquired a great deal of miscellaneous information; he went across into the Russian zone on several occasions and returned unmolested, which is quite easy if one looks miserable enough; he even took to following to their private haunts any man or woman who, he thought, looked tough and conscienceless enough to be their associates, whereby he ran far greater risks than ever he did from the Russians, but he found not the slightest trace of Gruiter or Ackermann.

"I think we're at a dead end here," said Hambledon. "We'd much better go back to Königswinter and ask the Fraulein Anna Knipe a few searching questions."

"There is something here, in Berlin," said Spelmann

80

passionately. "I feel it here." And he patted his fourth waistcoat button. "When I feel it here, it is so."

"My own diaphragm," said Hambledon, "is devoid of inspiration at the moment. Besides, I'm getting bored. Besides again, this looks like being a common or garden jewel robbery, even though there is nothing either common or garden about the jewels. You don't want me, you want your own excellent, highly trained, intelligent, and incorruptible police. They will do the work not only as well as I, but far better; it's their job, it's not mine. Call up your minions and let's go home. I have a home, believe it or not, and it's in London, not Berlin. I prefer London. Let's go and have one more glass of *Drachensblut* at the Im Tubac at Königswinter——"

"One more day," pleaded Spelmann. "Just one more day."

"Very well," said Tommy, looking at his watch. "Another twenty-four hours, and if you haven't produced a rabbit or so out of your hat by then, I shall ring up the airport and start packing my shirts."

"That is the trouble," said Spelmann sadly. "These people are not rabbits." He rubbed the peak of his cap to encourage a little more of the stiffening to show through the worn cloth, adjusted it at a despondent angle, and went out into the sunset.

There were two young men of Berlin's underworld also setting out upon their evening prowl at about that time. They had no particular object in view that night except the one object which they had always before them, money; and any method of getting it, from calling a taxi to breaking a bank, seemed equally good to them.

Some hours later, they were strolling together along a street near the Eastern zone border and stopped at a corner to look about them; their attitude was idle enough but their eyes and ears were busy.

A tall, thin man, reasonably well dressed and carrying an obviously full brief case, came along the pavement and turned the corner at which they were standing. He glanced at them in passing and went on. The young men looked at his brief case and at each other and turned, without a word, to follow him. Before they had started, two more men came by the way the first had come and also turned the corner; they were so busy talking to each other that they took no notice at all of the young hoodlums on the pavement but merely brushed past and hurried on. Their voices were low, but audible enough for the young men to recognize the language though they could not understand the words.

"Russkis," said one out of the corner of his mouth in the approved manner. The other nodded and they fell in behind. Something profitable can occasionally be done about Russians in the Western zone. So the little company proceeded; one tall man in front, striding easily, two Russians hurrying after him, and two Berlin thugs following them.

Spelmann, who had been lounging in a doorway looking forlorn and watching the Berliners, murmured something under his breath and drifted unhurriedly behind. He had a long stride for his height and walked faster than one would think to look at him.

Further along the street, ahead of the tall man, there was a check point in operation. This consisted, informally but quite efficiently, of four or five policemen standing in a group watching the passers-by and stopping one and another with a request to see their papers. These would be given up, scanned, and returned with a word of thanks, after which the owner would go his way. Check points are put into operation in Berlin frequently as a matter of routine; they are a help in picking up people of no known address who may have something useful to say, they are useful in providing information about newcomers to the city, and sometimes a big fish swims carelessly into the net.

Spelmann crossed the road to the opposite pavement and quickened his pace, the better to see what happened. The tall man saw the police and put his hand in an inside pocket for his papers, if required, as unconcernedly as a season-ticket traveller producing his pass for the eight-fifteen every morning. The two Russians also saw the police, hesitated momentarily, and vanished into doorways. It was done so quickly that Spelmann blinked; they were and then they were not. The two young Berliners slackened their pace to a stroll and crossed the road to Spelmann's side; this time they were behind him.

The tall man came up to the check point and stopped at once when one of the police addressed him.

"Your papers, please, mein Herr."

"Certainly," said the tall man. He gave them up with a smile and stood waiting calmly for their return. The police constable who had taken them gave them to the sergeant for examination, he unfolded them and looked attentively at them. Spelmann loitered along the opposite pavement and the two Berliners stopped to light cigarettes.

The police sergeant came forward, papers in hand. What he said was inaudible, but the tall man's voice was clear and carrying and his words were plain to hear.

"What? Nonsense. How dare you stop me?"

The police sergeant was understood to say that something or other was "no use," but the tall man persisted and two constables closed on him, one on either hand.

"I am Gustav Renzow," said the tall man, "on my way to American Headquarters. You will regret this."

Spelmann, now abreast, stopped dead, and the two Berlin youths joined him on the edge of the pavement. One of the police attempted to take the tall man's brief case from his hand, he resisted energetically and there was something of a struggle. Other passers-by naturally became interested and a small crowd, including Spelmann and the youths, formed round the combatants. The struggle was too one sided to last; the brief case was handed to the sergeant, and the two constables held the prisoner firmly by both arms.

"This is an outrage. I will complain to the——"

"I merely obey my orders, mein Herr, which are to arrest and detain for questioning any person carrying the

83

papers of Gustav Renzow. If there has been a mistake in identity, it will be corrected at the police station. Schmidt, ring through for the van."

The prisoner was hustled into an archway behind the sergeant and Constable Schmidt went into action with a walkie-talkie wireless set. The sergeant turned his back upon the crowd, opened the brief case, and plunged his hand into it. His formal gesture towards privacy was made ineffectual by the street lamp over his head; it was quite obvious that what he was pulling out were neat, fat bundles of Western zone notes.

He became aware, as if by telepathy, of the passionate interest which the crowd was taking in his proceedings, for he pushed the bundles back into the case, turned upon his audience, and asked them quite politely to go away. One cheerful old woman said she was in no hurry, if any of that stuff was being given away she'd wait all night; the sergeant grinned at her, the police van drove up with a flourish, and the crowd scattered. Spelmann looked about him for the two German youths but they had disappeared.

They were walking rapidly away, talking in low tones only when there was no one within earshot.

"Who was that? Bart Lachmann?"

"Don't know. Don't know him. But, what I've heard, he'd never let himself be took up like that."

"All that money!"—in a kind of wail—"Them police to 'ave it!"

The other groaned. "Best go and tell Gruiter——"

"Don't know where he lives."

"Best go and tell Ackie, then. Might be somethink in it for us."

They hurried through the streets to the semi-basement room where Ackermann lived. It was not far away; the same room in which Gruiter, Ackermann, Claussen, and Edberg had discussed with Lachmann his journey into Russia with Renzow's aeroplane designs. Ackermann himself opened the door; his wife, who was juggling with three saucepans on a small oilstove in the corner, looked over her shoulder at the visitors and the corners of her mouth went down when she saw who they were.

"Ernst and Heinz! Come in and welcome!"

They sidled in with muttered greetings to which Frau Ackermann did not reply; she bent over her stove and rattled potlids. There was a moment's awkward silence.

"We've seen something," said Ernst at last, "as we thought you ought to know about." His eyes slid round towards the woman in the corner.

"Klara!" said Ackermann.

"Yes, Hans."

"Go out for a walk."

"What, now, when I'm just in the middle of——"

"Get out!"

She began to obey in a frightened hurry, struggling unaided into a coat which she snatched off a nail, and pinning on askew a shapeless hat while Ackermann watched her with an air of sardonic amusement. At the last moment she remembered the cooking, stooped to turn the lamp out, and suddenly rebelled.

"It's too bad! Why can't you go out? Just when for once I've got a nice bit o' meat it's a pleasure to cook, and I've got to be turned out of my own kitchen for them two blackguards I wouldn't have had inside the house in the old days when——"

Ackermann pulled her towards him with one hand and struck her across the face with the other. She staggered back and upset the pots, their contents spreading and mingling on the floor.

"And don't cry. I don't like it. You know what 'appens when you do what I don't like, don't you? Get out!"

She clutched her coat about her, dodged round the table, and rushed out of the room.

"Pity about the supper," said Heinz hungrily.

"She can do it up again when she comes back. Never let up with women, that's the secret. Never let up. Now then, what's your news?"

They told him what they had seen, and he listened in

85

silence, his thick lower lip protruding and one fist softly thumping the table.

"And you don't know if it was Lachmann or not?" he said when they had finished.

"We don't know Lachmann, Ackie."

"Oh, don't you. What was he like, this man?"

But a description which conveyed a picture was quite beyond their powers. The man wasn't fat, he was what you'd call thin. He wasn't short either. A bit on the tall side as you might say. No, they didn't know the colour of his hair; he had a hat on, and they hadn't seen his face, not really. Actually, they hadn't taken that much notice till they saw all that money and then it was too late. He was nicely dressed and spoke haughty, like a toff.

"Bart putting on an act," nodded Ackermann. "That's him all right. Letting 'imself get roped in with all that money! We've got to do something, quick. Let me think——"

"Where's Gruiter?" asked Ernst.

"Be in any minute," said Ackermann. "We've got to do something tonight while Bart's still at that police station. Once they move 'im into a real jug, we're sunk. Shut up and let me think."

At about this time Spelmann was being whirled to the door of Hambledon's hotel in a taxi and was lucky enough to catch him standing upon the doorstep.

"Come with me," gasped Spelmann, seizing him by the arm and pushing him into the taxi. "Your rabbits are loose. Back to where we came from," he added to the driver as the door slammed. "Five rabbits, all running about! Well, not all. The police have caught one and en-hutched him."

"Let us abandon metaphor," said Tommy mildly.

"Very well." Spelmann described what he had seen. "I missed the two men I was following in the crowd; when the van moved off they were not there, so I waited about hoping to see the two Russians. I did not know they were Russians then, of course, not till I heard them talking. I do really think," said Spelmann anxiously, "that

86

what they were talking was Russian, not Polish. Does the Herr understand Polish?"

"I get the general gist of what is said. Where are they now?"

"They are in a café, it is crowded so they must wait to be served. Just round the next corner. Driver! Stop here, please."

"Spelmann," said Hambledon, getting out of the taxi after his energetic friend, "you say you were not very near the man who was arrested and never saw his face. Are you quite sure that he was not Gruiter?"

"Quite sure. Nothing like him. Different height, different shape. There they are, at that table at the back near the pillar."

Hambledon looked at them carefully to make sure that he had never met them before and then led the way into the café. A waiter indicated a vacant table near the radio which was energetically transmitting dance music, but Tommy shook his head and said he would prefer a quieter corner. Some people at a table next to the Russians' were preparing to go; he and Spelmann waited nearby until the places were vacant and then slid into them before anyone else could take them.

"It is good to sit down," said Hambledon, hoping that the Russians behind him could understand German. "I find your city tiring. I prefer my own Cologne, although I must admit I have done very well here."

"But you said, did you not, that you had finished your business here?" said Spelmann, playing up admirably. "Tomorrow you go home, do you not?"

"That is right. I have one more builder to see in the morning and then I have a seat booked on the 'plane. Next month I hope to be sent to Paris."

"Paris," said Spelmann enviously. "I would like to go there. I have never been. Have you?"

"Once, before the war. They tell me that the prices of everything there now are simply frightful. Where's the waiter? What will you have? Beer?"

"Beer, please. Can you speak French?"

87

"Oh yes," said Hambledon proudly, "quite well. It is a great advantage to have even one foreign language; I only wish I had more."

"There you are," said one of the Russians behind them in his own language. "You will not have understood that, but I did. They have just admitted that they are not sufficiently educated to understand us. We can speak freely."

"I mistrusted the people who sat at that table before," said the other. "When you mentioned 'a large sum of money' they looked round."

"That is why I mentioned it," said the first complacently. "To discover whether they understood Russian."

"You were always quick-witted, Andrei Ivanovich."

"I shall need to be," said Ivanovich gloomily, "to get Zolbin out of this mess."

"We ought to have contacted him before he left the Russian zone and stayed with him to protect him."

"But we were only told to shadow him and see where he went. Even now," said Ivanovich with a bitter laugh, "we have not lost him. We know where he is."

"In the police station, together with the money. What can we do about that, two men alone?"

There was a miserable silence which Hambledon and Spelmann filled by squabbling amiably about who was going to pay for the beer.

"There is only one thing to do," said Ivanovich with despairing determination. "Break into the police station, rescue Zolbin, and seize the money."

"But we shall immediately be killed!"

"Let me ask you, Vassily, what you suppose will happen to us if we go home without all that money and leaving him behind? Do you expect to be given the Order of Lenin, a certificate for first-class rations, and a three-roomed flat? It's no use moaning like a sick cow, Vassily Andreyevich, we must face facts. They may be unpleasant, but they are not yet a post in an execution shed. Here, we have a chance."

"But—to attack a police station!"

"Listen, Vassily, and pull yourself together. Have you

ever considered that, of all the buildings in a city, the only one of which the front door is never locked is a police station? Well, it's true. There, you're feeling better already, aren't you? We wait until about two o'clock and they are all asleep or drowsy and then we walk in. There will be a man at the desk, him we will shoot at once. Then, while you stand in the passage and shoot down anyone who comes out of any of the rooms, I take the keys, unlock the cell doors till I find Zolbin, and let him out. Then we take the money and go out with him."

"How many police will there be in the station?"

"The man at the desk. One sergeant and two—possibly three but probably only two—constables. If you are ready to put a bullet into anyone who shows his nose round a doorpost, Vassily, the thing is as good as done."

"And where will the money be?"

"If I know anything, it will be in the desk for tonight, probably still in his brief case. Just a simple wooden desk such as we had at school, Vassily, with a simple lock on it. You kick it and the thing falls to pieces. On my word, Vassily Andreyevich, I'm quite looking forward to this. I'm going to enjoy it, and think of the reward we shall get when we go back!"

Vassily shifted uncomfortably. "I do not altogether like this plan, Comrade. It leaves too much to chance."

"Then suggest a better!"

"There is a great deal of money there. Would it not be possible to reason with the station sergeant and offer him the money in exchange for the person of Vadim Zolbin? If the police records were expunged, there would be no trace of his arrest."

"And what do you suppose the station sergeant will be doing while you unfold your pretty scheme? Sucking his thumb like a baby? Besides, to whom does the money belong which you are proposing to give away in handfuls? It is the property of the Soviet, and you are suggesting we should use it to save ourselves a little trouble. Let me suggest to you, Comrade Vassily Andreyevich, that such talk isn't at all healthy for you."

"For heaven's sake, Andrei Ivanovich! I thought you were a friend to whom I could speak frankly what was in my mind."

"Of course I am your friend, too good a friend to allow you to go on harbouring the sort of poisonous nonsense you have just uttered. Pull yourself together—as I had to tell you only just now, did I not?—and stop making this ridiculous fuss about a simple operation. Relax, Vassily Andreyevich, relax. Have another drink, such as it is. Steinhager, they call it. Oh for a glass of our good native vodka! I know what's the matter with you, you're missing your vodka and I don't wonder at it; I do, too. Here, waiter! Two Steinhagers, and be quick about it, please. It is now one o'clock, we will have our little drink and then stroll quietly off to survey the scene of our imminent victory. Cheer up! In two hours' time it will be all over and we can go home again, happy in the knowledge that we have done our duty. Here's your drink, down with it! Your health and long life to you, Vassily, my old friend."

They emptied their glasses and swaggered out; the moment they were gone Hambledon and Spelmann rose up to follow them through the dark streets.

9 TEMPERANCE ADVOCATE

"What were they saying?" asked Spelmann.

Hambledon told him. "You know this is really beginning to be quite interesting," he added. "Here is a Russian named Vadim Zolbin who is carrying Renzow's personal papers. He is being helpfully pursued by those two ornaments of hell ahead of us because, apparently, he is also carrying a large sum of money. What's the money for, Spelmann?"

"To buy the Renzow aircraft designs, of course."

"I think so, too. So the designs are somewhere in Berlin. This fellow Zolbin was going to meet somebody, no doubt. What a pity the police arrested him; if you'd been able to follow him home, we might have had the designs in our hands by now. It's rather odd, don't you think, that he was carrying Renzow's papers? How is Renzow?"

"Still unconscious, I heard today. But, since Zolbin thought himself safe in using Renzow's papers, the question I ask myself is: Where does he think Renzow is? I answer myself: Somewhere where he cannot protest. We can take it that he knows who Renzow is. Look out, they are looking back."

"Turn left," said Hambledon. "We can rejoin this road further on. Oh yes, Renzow is a famous man and you can bet the Russians know all about him, especially anyone with any connection with aircraft."

"But they can't know he's in hospital as a result of a murderous assault, or this man would not have attempted to impersonate him."

"No," said Hambledon slowly. "You are quite right there, Spelmann. It looks very much as though they thought he was dead."

"What—in hospital?"

"No, no. Listen. Renzow's personal papers have been in Russian territory. Who took them there?"

"One of Gruiter's gang," said Spelmann. "Or, more likely, whoever it was who employed them to steal the designs."

"I am not sure that anyone did. I think they went to Königswinter after the jewels and just took the designs as well on the chance they might be valuable. No, I don't mean what *individual* was it who went across the border with the designs and papers. I mean, what did he call himself?"

"Gustav Renzow, of course—of course! The papers would take him into the Russian zone all right. It was when this man Zolbin tried to use them in the British sector that he ran into trouble."

"Yes. I think the substitute Renzow who went over to the Russians must be dead. Or in a Russian jail, which is much the same thing."

"I think so, too. And all that money—" said Spelmann.

"There they are again," interrupted Hambledon. "Don't let them see us. They're stopping; take cover!"

Before them stretched a wide and empty road, on the right it was flat and open where ruined buildings had been cleared away and sites for new buildings laid out. In one place a start had been made, for hoardings surrounded a skeleton of steel framing. Across the road there was a row of houses in reasonably good condition; one of them was a police station with the door, as Ivanovich had prophesied, standing open. The Russians were inconspicuous against a corner of the hoarding; it was not possible unobserved to get near enough to hear what they were saying, but they were talking earnestly together.

"Comrade Andrei Ivanovich delivering another of his pep talks," said Hambledon.

"And Comrade Vassily Andreyevich still doesn't like the look of things."

" 'But screw your courage to the sticking place . . .' They're off! No, they're not; they've changed their minds. Why?"

"There's someone coming up the other way," said Spelmann, who from his place could see a little further past the hoarding than Hambledon could. "Three men. Two policemen and a prisoner between them. And a fourth man behind, not in uniform."

"These reinforcements will postpone the Russian onslaught, surely. Besides, they'll wake the police out of their midnight drowse, no longer to be caught nap—— I say, what a funny prisoner! He's so eager to get jugged that he's ahead of his captors."

"The police are a little queer, too. The one this side. I know we can't be too fussy about recruits these days, but he's unusually short. In the Bonn police, we——"

"And his trousers don't fit him," said Hambledon. "Either they're too long, or they're coming down. Look, he's hitching them up with his spare hand. You can't hitch up trousers with only one hand; someone ought to tell him."

"They've gone in, anyway. And the plain-clothes man, too. Now what happens?"

Nothing at all happened for what seemed a long time, but was possibly five minutes. The two Russians stayed where they were and so did Hambledon and Spelmann. The streets were empty at that hour, and the traffic of Berlin had ceased for the night. From one of the houses across the road there came the sound of a child crying loudly and the cry rose to the scream of nightmare. At once a light sprang up in a window, the cries died down and ceased and a silent peace drifted down like snow over that area of Berlin.

It was abruptly shattered by a voice shouting inside the police station; the voice stopped abruptly when a shot was fired. Immediately more shouting broke out and more shooting followed——

The two alleged constables were Ackermann's hoodlum friends, Ernst and Heinz, who had seen Zolbin arrested, and their alleged prisoner was Bruno Gruiter. The civilian walking behind the three was Ackermann himself. They entered the police station to find themselves in a wide passage with two closed doors on the right and the desk sergeant's throne on the left. At the far end, the passage turned to the right; round this corner were the four cells.

The desk sergeant looked up when the company of four entered. He did not know the constables personally, but that did not surprise him; he could not know the whole of the Berlin police force, and if two of them had run down a wanted man outside their own area they would naturally bring him in to whatever police station happened to be nearest. He stifled a yawn and stretched out his arm for his record book, thinking only that this was the fourth prisoner brought in that night; if any more came in they must go two in a cell. He picked up his pen as the party reached his desk and looked up to see a large revolver in the hands of the alleged prisoner, and it was pointed straight at his chest.

"Quiet, no noise," said the prisoner softly. "The cell keys, quick."

"Gruiter!" gasped the sergeant. "I haven't got them."

He also spoke in a low tone. How right was Damon Runyon to call a gun "the old persuader."

"Oh yes, you 'ave. I knows the drill, you've put me away often enough." Gruiter spoke boldly enough, but actually the instant recognition had shaken him badly; his face was white and glistening and his hands trembled. It was a piece of unexpected bad luck to encounter a policeman who could recognize him on sight. Ackermann saw his uneasiness and took charge.

"They're chained to 'is belt. Get up, you ——, and do what you're told or you'll get it." Ackermann went behind the desk and the sergeant rose to his feet, for he was a family man and did not wish to die. He was urged along the passage with Gruiter prodding him in the back with the revolver, largely to give himself courage.

"Which cell's he in?" asked Heinz, and Ackermann glanced contemptuously at him.

"Don't matter. Let 'em all out. May as well."

The desk sergeant opened the first cell he came to, and, as though he were a runner poised at the starting line, Zolbin dashed out and along the passage. He was not Lachmann so Ackermann naturally let him go; without his overcoat Ernst and Heinz did not recognize him and in any case were relying upon Ackermann to identify his friend. The next cell door opened to reveal a drunk who stared haughtily at them and was in no hurry to go; the third door released a thin young man who had been caught in the very act of burglary only an hour before.

The fourth cell was empty and its door was already open.

"Where is he?" asked Ackermann, but the desk sergeant turned like an eel behind them to make a rush for the corner, with a loud yell to alarm his colleagues in the rest rooms off the passage. Gruiter, having been already recognized and seeing as it were an embodied report rushing to the inspector, lost his head and fired. The crash of the shot rang along the corridor and the bullet hit the desk sergeant in the back of the head, killing him instantly.

In a moment the place was in an uproar. The two constables drowsing in the rest room, not actually on duty but "on call" in case they were needed, made a leap for the door just as they were, in shirt and trousers, pausing only to snatch up their belts with the holsters containing their automatics. It is not at all easy to get a gun out of a holster on a belt which is merely swinging in the hand, and they were still fumbling when they came out to be faced by a tall man who had wrenched open the lid of the sergeant's desk. He had a bulging brief case in one hand and a piece of the broken lid in the other, with this he struck in the face the first constable to oppose him and immediately rushed out of the door into the night.

The inspector was reading reports in his room and trying to keep awake when the cry and the shot outside awoke him effectively. He too snatched up his gun and opened his door at the exact moment when what seemed like the hordes of Attila galloped past, headed by the thin burglar, with Ackermann and his three friends close upon his heels. Gruiter fired his revolver again at the inspector's face and missed, the bullet sang past his ear and the hot wind scorched his cheek. The two constables by this time had got their guns out, but in the excitement of the moment were firing high, and the whole battle emerged upon the street.

The first that Hambledon and Spelmann actually saw of what was happening was when the door of the police station erupted the tall man, running like a hare away from them with his brief case clutched to his chest.

"That's him," said Spelmann excitedly. "Zolbin."

The Russians leapt from cover, waving their arms and crying: "Zolbin! Comrade!" Zolbin glanced over his shoulder and evidently saw them, but instead of stopping he put his head down and ran harder than ever. The Comrades, after a momentary pause of astonishment, set off after him, yelping: "Stop, stop," but he did not stop. Flight and pursuit disappeared into the distance.

There was an angry exodus from the police station, headed by Ackermann and closely followed by the station staff and their inspector who had seen his dead ser-

95

geant and was bellowing to his constables to "shoot to kill." The inspector himself steadied his arm against the jamb of the door, took careful aim at Gruiter as he was running away, and fired. Gruiter leapt in the air and fell in a heap, moving feebly.

"One," said the inspector grimly.

By this time both constables were firing from such cover as they could find and Ackermann's gang were firing back. It was at this moment that the police-station door emitted another figure, and he was carrying a chair. He pushed past the inspector, who was too busy to stop him, advanced into the middle of the road, set down his chair, and mounted upon it. He was the drunken prisoner from Cell 2,. and he had a message to deliver; regardless of flying bullets, the crash of shots, and the yells and imprecations of battle he proceeded to deliver it.

"People of Berlin, take warning! Berlin is a sink of iniquity like Gorram and Somoddah. Evil is rampant. What is the evil of which I speak? Drink."

He had the high, carrying voice of the practised orator; though his words were often entangled they were always perfectly audible, and his remarks floated across to Hambledon at all times when he had attention to spare for them.

"Look around you. What do you see? A bagglefiel'—a battlefound——"

The young burglar, having been searched on arrest, was unarmed and decided suddenly to leave. He had the intelligence or the experience to run zigzag, and finally put on a spurt to pass close by Hambledon, who stuck his leg out. The burglar, having his feet swept from under him, fell heavily, hitting his head upon a lump of masonry, and lay very still.

The voice of the speaker continued without pause. ". . . Whose degraded body lies yonder in a drunken stupor"—he was referring to Gruiter who was as dead as Argentine beef—"is a victim of the devil whose alternated nomacl—nomenacl—name is Steinhager and Beer, alternately. Oh, my friends——"

96

Ernst had received a bullet in the chest and was on the ground, trying to drag himself away in the intervals of coughing his heart out. The inspector had been wounded in the leg by Ackermann and was sitting on the steps cursing steadily and waiting for Heinz to move out from behind a tree opposite.

"Where did this graceful orgy take place? I will tell——"

Heinz did move eventually, since the constables were working round towards him; he had fired off the contents of his magazine and was too agitated to reload. The inspector, who rightly prided himself upon his revolver shooting, chose the moment when Heinz came out from behind the tree and dropped him. He was not dead but, as the constables told him when they picked him up, that did not matter; the postponement was only temporary.

"Within those doors labelled 'Polizei,' sheens of the most unexscribeable dishipation take place hourly. I know. I have but now escaped——"

Ackermann had kept his head. After emptying his automatic in the general direction of the police and scoring upon the inspector, he ran down the side of the builder's hoarding and was lost to sight.

The two Russians, with but one idea in both their minds and one duty clear before them, had ignored the battle completely. In fact, after the first few minutes they were not there, for they were running furiously along the road after Zolbin. He, being taller than either of his pursuers, would normally have outdistanced them easily, but he was hampered by his brief case. Track records are not broken while clasping a sizeable satchel stuffed with bundles of Deutschmark notes and other things. He gained a little but not much, and was in the act of glancing over his shoulder to see how far off they were when an elderly man came out of a side street upon a bicycle and Zolbin ran straight into him. There was a loud crash and two men and bicycle rolled together in the road.

Zolbin picked up himself, the brief case, and the bicycle

97

almost in one movement, sprang on the machine and was away down the side turning before his pursuers could reach him. His progress was not, at first, easy because the handlebars had been twisted round until they were no longer at right angles with the front wheel. However, he had been a good cyclist in the days when, as a young man, he had worked in Germany, and he managed to lose the pursuit. He got off, hurriedly effected an adjustment, and rode anxiously away into the night. He had not been caught, but he was most hopelessly and comprehensively lost.

The elderly man whose bicycle had been reft from him struggled to his feet as the other Russians came up panting, and seized them by their coats.

"Who took my bike?"

"We—I—it wasn't us," said Ivanovich in his limited German, and pulled to get away.

"I know it weren't you, but you was running after 'im. Friend o' yours?"

"No," said Ivanovich loudly. "Certainly not. I don't know him. Let go, old man, or I——"

"Then why was you running after?"

Ivanovich searched a treacherous memory for the German word for "coincidence," and failed to find it. "Life is like that," he said at last. "Let go, or I will strike you."

"I will tell the police," said the old man. He pushed them peevishly away and they also disappeared down the side street which Zolbin had taken, but sadly and in no hurry. Zolbin had gone and all they needed now was a quiet place in which to consider.

"Life," said Vassily Andreyevich passionately, "is unnecessarily cruel."

The old man plodded on towards the police station where everything was now peaceful once more. The firing had entirely ceased, and all the neighbours had come out of their houses to stand about asking questions and uttering cries of horror when they encountered pools of blood in the road. Heinz was carried in, moaning loudly; Ernst also, but he did not moan because he was as dead as Gruiter. Police reinforcements arrived, and Hambledon indicated the person of the burglar.

"I didn't hit him," he explained. "I thought you might want him for something so I only tripped him up."

The police rolled the burglar over. "He's all right," they said. "Only stunned. He'll wake up again in an hour's time, back in his little cell. He will be disappointed, won't he?"

The crowd had surged forwards towards the police station, from the steps of which the inspector had at last consented to be removed for bandaging, and the police had a moment to spare to attend to the orator. His head, which had been visible above the crowd, disappeared suddenly but his voice continued as he was borne away, until it died into the distance along the passage towards the cells.

"Even the inspector cannot stand up, he has to cling to doorposts——"

Hambledon came up to the crowd, who were laughing loudly in reaction to the recent horrors, and asked who on earth that was.

"A temperance advocate——"

"So I heard!"

"But only when he is drunk, mein Herr. When he is sober he sells picture postcards."

Hambledon pushed his way through the crowd towards the police station, and was himself elbowed back in the doorway by an elderly man with a just grievance. He stamped along the passage and laid hold upon a sergeant.

"I have a complaint to make. A serious and important complaint."

"What's the matter?" asked the sergeant, abstracting his mind with difficulty from two dead prisoners, a wounded inspector, and the shrouded form of the desk sergeant who had been his friend for many years. Someone would have to go and tell his wife. "What's your trouble?"

"I've lost my bike."

The sergeant laughed.

Vadim Zolbin was, like Gustav Renzow, an aircraft designer. In 1933 his father was labelled a "Trotsky-deviationist," and disappeared into the Lubianka prison in Moscow never to be heard of again. Vadim was an only child and his mother was dead; he had, therefore, no one to consider but himself; he was then twenty years old and had seen quite enough of Soviet methods to know that, being his father's son, there was not much future for him in Russia. The Soviet authorities do not pay overmuch heed to the doctrines of the Bible but there is one text which they do most earnestly observe, that which says that "the sins of the fathers shall be visited on the children."

Vadim left Russia and wandered across Europe, doing whatever work would provide him with food and shelter. He had had the beginnings of an engineering training and more than a natural bent for it; when he obtained work in the drawing office of the Focke-Wulf works at Bremen, he knew he had found his place in the world. Here he met Gustav Renzow, and indeed, worked under him. Zolbin rose rapidly in his profession and was generally regarded as a "coming man," when in 1939 Hitler signed a treaty of alliance with Soviet Russia.

There is little doubt that Germany made a complete fool of the U.S.S.R. in this treaty; it was partly to insure against the war-on-two-fronts which Germany always dreaded, and partly to draw upon Russia's illimitable supplies of raw materials. There had to be a few counterbalancing clauses to benefit Russia, if only for the look of the thing; one of them specified the return to Russia of such of her nationals as were of scientific or technical value. Vadim Zolbin unwillingly returned to his native land.

It is a measure of his technical brilliance that he was still alive and reasonably prosperous, for his political background was suspect and he never felt himself safe.

On no less than three occasions he had been called to the M.V.D. Headquarters for one of their "little talks," and each time he knew very well that only his value to the aircraft industry had preserved him from disaster. The dramatic success of the MIG-15, in the design of which he had had a large share, set him above mischance for some time, but he was beginning to feel that its effect was wearing thin and no man can go on producing new and better MIGs indefinitely. Besides, he was homesick for a civilized way of life; decent clothes, decent housing, and, above all, decent police.

When Lachmann arrived in the Soviet zone with his photostats of the Renzow designs, he was sent to Zolbin at Minsk, near the Polish frontier, to be interviewed and have the photographs examined. Minsk was a reasonably convenient place to which to take Lachmann since it was only about fourteen hours from Berlin; Zolbin worked there and he spoke fluent technical German. He was, besides, perfectly capable of assessing the value of aircraft designs and particularly capable, Moscow thought, of judging these since he had worked under Renzow in the past and knew his habits of mind. When Zolbin was told that Gustav Renzow had come over to sell his latest designs to the U.S.S.R., he did not quite believe it but neither did he argue. One does not, if a Soviet citizen, argue with Moscow.

The moment that Zolbin saw Lachmann, therefore, he knew that the alleged Renzow was a fraud. Lachmann refused to talk aeroplanes at all, saying that he was in a hurry, there was no time to waste. He took a high hand with Zolbin as he had done with all those whom he had interviewed earlier upon this journey. There were the designs, and his price was half a million marks in Western zone currency. Take it or leave it. He tilted his hat to the back of his head and lit a cigarette.

Zolbin assumed quite correctly that these designs had been stolen but he was not in the least concerned. If Renzow could not take better care of his designs he deserved to lose them, and so long as they came into Russian hands it did not matter who brought them. He looked attentively at the photographs, producing a small magnifying glass from his pocket to see them in greater detail. They covered, it will be remembered, only a quarter of each sheet, but there was enough there for him to see what Renzow had been driving at and he was intensely interested. He had himself made some study of the problem of varying in flight the angle of sweep of swept-back wing aircraft and had found the difficulties insoluble. But Renzow, whose reputation had risen with the years, might have found solutions which had evaded Zolbin.

He put the photographs down and looked at Lachmann.

"These photostats appear to be of some interest," said Zolbin coldly. "I should, of course, have to see the whole sheets before deciding whether they are, in fact, worth even a small fraction of the absurdly large sum you mentioned."

"Then I'm afraid you won't, mister; and my figure is what I said. Five hundred thousand Western marks."

"Ridiculous," said Zolbin.

"They're worth that to you Russians," said Lachmann obstinately. "You aren't bargaining for stale fish on a Saturday night, you know. This is something that'll put your air force on top of the world, and you know it. All I'm asking for it is less than a fortnight's wages for a biggish factory. I can't think what's the matter with me. Mister, I'm giving them away."

If the designs were all they seemed, this was nearly true.

"You had better remember," said Zolbin in a menacing tone, "that you are miles inside Russia and completely in our power."

To do Lachmann justice, he was not easily intimidated. He grinned in Zolbin's face and said: "But the designs aren't. Do you want the Western powers to have 'em? True, they won't pay so much as you, that's why I come here first, but they'll pay if only to keep 'em out of your hands. Look, you're not only buying the designs, you're paying me not to let them have 'em. It 'ud be cheap at

102

half a million marks for you to see me burn 'em."

"How am I to know you aren't selling them to both sides as it is?"

Lachmann was deeply hurt, and said so. "Mister, though you don't seem to know it, there is such a thing as commercial honesty——"

"I know there is," said Zolbin crisply. "What I question is whether you practise it. However, I am empowered to offer you one hundred thousand marks."

"Five hundred thousand. What I said."

They argued about the price and eventually settled for three hundred thousand marks which was exactly the figure Lachmann had suggested to Gruiter and his associates at their first meeting. Lachmann was delighted but naturally did not show it.

"Where are the designs?" asked Zolbin.

"In Berlin. This is what you have to do. You send a man with the money with me to Berlin. I take him to the house of a friend of mine. The designs aren't there, but when my friend sees the money he'll go and get them. Then your man can hand over the money and we'll hand over the drawings."

"Or knock him on the head and keep both money and designs," said Zolbin. "Do you take me for a child? You will stay here as a hostage for your friends' good behaviour, and when the designs are safely received here you can go home."

Lachmann argued, but Zolbin remained unmoved and eventually the German gave in. He was removed to safekeeping; when he found it was simply a jail he protested bitterly, but no one took the least notice. Zolbin communicated the results of his interview to his superiors in Moscow and received in reply orders to go to Berlin himself, since he was the only German-speaking man available with enough technical knowledge to know whether the series of drawings he would be offered were both genuine and complete. Zolbin, as it happened, had not heard that Renzow was in hospital with a serious brain injury, but the news had already reached Moscow. They

103

deduced from it that they would be quite safe in buying what might well be his last designs for some time if not forever, provided that the sale was exclusively to Russia. Zolbin was told to make sure that the drawings were the originals and not copies, and, if possible, to find out whether copies had been made before the originals, if they were originals, had been offered for sale to Russia.

Normally Zolbin would have torn his hair over the typically bureaucratic idiocy of the last paragraph; but, though he ran his eyes over it, he did not at all take in the sense—if any—for a blindingly brilliant idea had come upon him. Ever since he had been sent back to Russia in 1939, he had wanted to get out again; and here, handed him on a plate by his office in Moscow, was his supreme chance. He was being sent, actually and officially sent, into the Western sector of Berlin with travel permits and passes all provided and three hundred thousand Western marks in his pocket.

He got up and walked about the room, for fortunately he was alone. He sat down, wiped the perspiration of excitement from his forehead, and said to himself: "There is a catch in it somewhere." He thought the orders over carefully and could see no catch in them; what would almost certainly happen would be that a couple of men from the M.V.D.—the Gestapo of Russia—would be put on to follow him everywhere he went. He shrugged his shoulders at them, a little observation would tell him if he was being followed, and by whom; if he could not shake them off in Berlin he did not deserve to escape. As for the designs, anyone could have them; he had a better use for the money.

Berlin would not be a good place to stay in; it was an island in Soviet territory, and even if one remained carefully within the confines of the Western sector there was such a thing as kidnapping. However, one would deal with that when one came to it, and he looked at the neat bundles of Deutschmark notes.

Zolbin got up again from his chair and walked slowly up and down the room, thinking deeply. It was a habit of his to walk up and down if he had a problem to think out; when, therefore, his woman secretary opened the door and saw him doing this, she closed the door again softly and tiptoed away to tell the office staff to keep quiet and not chatter in the passages. The boss was working out something and they knew what would happen if they disturbed him. Zolbin saw her come and go and knew himself to be safe from interruption; he unlocked his safe and took from it four large sheets of designs, two of them not yet completed. They were large, about six feet by three and a half, but the paper was not very thick; they were rolled up, not folded. He looked at them undecidedly for a moment and then, making up his mind, folded each of them repeatedly until the resultant packet was little more than a foot square. He put each of them as it was done into his brief case and added the bundles of notes; the case bulged rather conspicuously so he put it upon his chair and sat upon it until the contents were flattened.

He took four rolls of discarded drawings from a chest and put them in his safe; they looked like the others unless they were unrolled. He hesitated again, looking at his brief case; if he were found to be carrying those designs he was done, but a moment later he threw back his head, went to the door, and called his secretary.

"Natasha Pavlovna, I have to go away for a few days. I shall be back as soon as possible, but it may be a week before I return. I leave this office in your care. The designs I am working on at the moment are in the safe, let no one touch them on your life."

"Take the keys with you, Comrade Zolbin, then no one can meddle with them."

"I was going to leave them with you——"

"No, take them with you. I would rather not have the responsibility."

"Very well." He dropped the keys in his pocket and picked up his hat. "Good-bye, Natasha Pavlovna, for a few days."

Zolbin went to the prison where Lachman was detained

and showed him the orders which had come from Moscow. It was only a gesture, for Lachmann could not read Russian, as Zolbin had guessed, so he obligingly translated the letter word by word. Lachmann was pleased, and said so.

"There you are, see? Your bosses in Moscow know a good offer when they see one."

"Yes, indeed," said Zolbin meekly.

"Only thing is, I'm not stopping in this hole while you go and come back. Why, it might be days if there was a hold-up in transport. I see your point about me being a hostage, though there's not the least need for it, me and my friends being gentlemen of their word——"

He paused, but Zolbin said nothing.

"But I'm staying in a hotel, not a lousy jail."

"Oh, certainly," said Zolbin. "I'll speak to the governor of this place on my way out and tell him to release you. It won't be till tomorrow probably, you won't mind one more night. I'm sorry," as Lachmann began to protest, "but there'll be stacks of forms to fill up in triplicate and get signed and countersigned. Red tape, you know, all red tape, but I'm afraid we've got rather a lot of it in Russia. You must excuse us."

"Oh, very well," said Lachmann unwillingly. "You might book a room for me at the hotel while you're about it; it is a bit awkward not speaking your language."

"Certainly," said Zolbin again. "I shall pass it when I leave here."

"What's it called?"

"The—er—the Star. In Hope Street. Quite close, you can almost see it from your window. Good-bye. I will see you when I return."

Zolbin left the cell and went to see the governor, a local man who stood in some awe of a man from Moscow.

"That German prisoner in Cell 47B," said Zolbin. "Take care of him, he may be wanted some day. Do not believe one word he says, he is a liar and a cheat, that is why he is here. By the way, you have his personal papers?"

"Certainly," said the governor, "certainly, Comrade. I have them filed in this cupboard—here they are. My filing system——"

"Excellent," said Zolbin, putting Lachmann's papers in his pocket. "Impeccable and beautifully kept, I am sure."

"But the papers," objected the governor. "A receipt is necessary, Comrade, if they are to be taken. I am sorry——"

"Hush!" said Zolbin imperiously. "It is a question for expert examination, if they are forged, you know. The utmost discretion until we have found out who gave them to him. You understand."

"But——"

"It is only for a couple of hours and you shall have them back. It is imperatively necessary that there should be no trace of their having been taken out."

The governor subsided and Zolbin walked away. He had had personal papers issued to him, but he wanted German ones and these were all he could get; they seemed to have served Lachmann very well. Zolbin went to the station and left Minsk by train for Berlin. It did not take him long to pick out the Comrades Andrei Ivanovich and Vassily Andreyevich as the two who had been appointed to watch over him, and he made no effort to shake them off on the journey, or when the train arrived at the Ost station in Berlin, or even when he changed into an underground train. The very last thing he wished to do was to give the slightest cause for suspicion on the Russian side. It was only when he came up to the surface in the Western sector that he began to quicken his pace and bend his mind upon shaking off his pursuers. He had, of course, not the slightest intention of even trying to get into contact with Lachmann's friend who held Renzow's designs; his one idea was to get clear away.

Ahead of him along the street there was a police checkpost and for a moment Zolbin caught his breath. However, it would not be wise to show fear, and he noticed that they were not stopping everyone. Why should they pick on him if he put a bold face on it? He strode unconcernedly on, feeling for his papers beforehand in the hope that a plain willingness to show them would obviate a demand for them. Even if they had to be shown they were perfectly good papers. . . .

But the police pounced on him at once, as has been said, and the only consolation Zolbin found in his predicament was the scandalized expression on the faces of the two M.V.D. men as he was swept away in the police car. At least he was out of their reach for the time being.

When Gruiter and his friends staged their attack upon the police station, Zolbin was pacing up and down his cell—three paces and turn, three paces and turn—trying to make up his mind what to say when he was interrogated in the morning. Probably the best way out of his difficulties would be to appeal for asylum as a political refugee, and he could add as inducements to mercy his own services as an aircraft designer and his own designs he had brought out with him, the address where Renzow's stolen designs could be found, and three hundred thousand Western marks. On the other hand, he was afraid to remain in Berlin. Acceptance as a political refugee is a slow business which may take weeks, and in the meantime he would be living in some sort of camp. The Russians would stop at nothing to get him back and they would certainly succeed, after which death would be a desired haven. No, it would be better not to apply for asylum. Again, he had been caught with Renzow's personal papers on him and instantly arrested, he had no idea why, and for all he knew Renzow might have been foully murdered and he would be accused of having been involved in it. Finally, there were those three hundred thousand marks in the sergeant's desk; they had been put there in his presence, and his soul hungered after them. His designs too, yes, but he had them in his head and could get them out again, probably with minor improvements, but the money, ah, the money! It meant safety, for with its help he could travel to the opposite side of the world from Russia; it meant security from want; in fact, it meant all the four freedoms to Vadim Zolbin, and he racked his brains to think of a scheme whereby he could retain it.

Suddenly, without warning, like a direct intervention of Providence in answer to prayer, his cell door was unlocked and he saw the desk sergeant being coerced by a man holding a revolver. Other men in the group glanced at him without interest and turned away, leaving the door open. Zolbin leapt out——

After he had shaken off the pursuit by Ivanovich and Andreyevich, he cycled on through the deserted streets of Berlin trying to find a landmark he recognized. But he had never known the city at all well, and as anyone knows who has visited, after heavy bombing, a town he once knew whole, the mere effort to recognize the unrecognizable is more confusing than total ignorance. He rode on, turning left or right to avoid the occasional policeman or night watchman, until he came unexpectedly upon a group of soldiers and saw that they were Russian. He had strayed back into the Soviet sector.

The soldiers took no notice of him. Why should they? He rode past them and took the next turning to be out of their sight. As soon as they could no longer see him, he dismounted from the bicycle and sat down upon a low wall because his legs were trembling and his heart thumping so violently that he found it difficult to breathe. He had always led a reasonably comfortable life with good clothes, regular meals, and a bed to sleep in every night; this was the first time he had been really "on the run," and panic had seized him. Everyone, he felt, must be looking for him and at any moment someone would come up to him and say: "Vadim Zolbin, you are under arrest." He broke into a violent perspiration; he could feel the drops of sweat trickling behind his ears.

Presently he pulled himself together and looked about him. He was in a slum street of mean houses whose ragged tenants still flitted about in the shadows, although it was,

109

by then, nearly three in the morning. He approached an old woman and asked her if she could let him have a room, he muttered something about having lost his train.

She looked sharply at him, shaking her head, then her face softened for she had seen frightened men before. She said he could have her son's bed, such as it was, and he could put his bicycle in the coal shed. Her son was away for a few nights, when he came back he must have his bed again——

Zolbin said: "Of course, of course," and did not breathe freely till he was within the house and the door shut behind him. The bed was merely a mattress on the floor and the place was not even clean, but at least he was under cover. He rolled his briefcase in his coat for a pillow and slept uneasily until daylight.

He stayed indoors all next day until it grew dark and his courage gradually returned to him. The old woman fed him upon a sort of vegetable stew, hot but not particularly nourishing, and talked about her son who had been in the German Army and won the Iron Cross, Third Class, for gallantry in Holland. "Every time he went away after he'd been on leave, my poor stomach, oh dear! I couldn't keep nothing down. And then mixed drafts, as they call them; all strange soldiers as didn't belong together. It wasn't as though he went away with friends; it seemed to make it worse, like——"

Zolbin had never been in the Army and had taken but little interest in its organization, but now that it was recalled to his mind he remembered going to Moscow station to see off a friend who was going to the front. That had been a "mixed draft," none of the soldiers knew each other, and the germ of a plan of escape began to form in his mind. After dark he went out for a prowl round the neighbourhood, but there were not many soldiers about and he returned to his squalid room for another night and day. After all there was no immediate hurry; if he did not return to report for a couple of days, it would merely be assumed that he had met with delay in obtaining Renzow's papers.

110

On the following night he went out again and this time he came upon a low café, noisy, dirty, and crowded with soldiers. He went in, sat down at a table, and ordered a glass of vodka. It was not good vodka, but the warmth of it ran through his veins; he ordered another and looked about him, listening attentively to the conversations.

Some of the soldiers were celebrating the fact that they were going home on leave and others were returning to duty; there was much loud laughter, some harmless horseplay, and a lot of jokes which would not have passed the most liberal-minded censor. Eventually Zolbin noticed in a corner a long, thin, melancholy soldier surrounded by items of equipment which he would be expected to festoon about his person; as though this were not enough he had added a balalaika to his burden and was strumming sadly upon it in the intervals between drinks. He was returning from leave to go back on duty and he did not like it. He said so.

"All very well for you, Comrades. You're all going home, if you've got a home. I've got a home; I've just been there on leave. Now where am I? Here. I don't want to be here."

"Cheer up, Piotr, cheer up. You aren't the only one."

"I'm going to Memel——"

"I'm off to Lodz——"

"And I'm for Bielitz——"

"I know, I know," said the melancholy Piotr. "You're all going to places among nice people who like us. People who talk something you can understand, even if it sounds a bit funny. But I'm going miles and miles and miles away on the West front all among the lousy Germans——"

"Cheer up, Comrade!"

"I won't cheer up. They don't like me; I don't like them."

Zolbin got up and went to the door, ostensibly to look out at the weather. When he came back someone had taken his seat so he went across to sit near Piotr.

"Can't understand one word they say."

"Then how d'you know they don't like you? Maybe they all love you!"

"They don't. They look rude."

"Oh, cut out the wails and give us a song!"

Piotr emptied a glass for which Zolbin had paid, struck a few arpeggios on his balalaika, and broke into the tune of "My Uncle's Parrot," an old song which Russian soldiers have been singing for years. "My Uncle" had a parrot with a homing instinct which would have done credit to any prize pigeon. When "My Uncle" became financially embarrassed he would take his parrot down to the market and barter it for flour or drink or an old overcoat. Then "My Uncle" would return home satisfied, but the parrot was always there before him. Eventually, however, the parrot came home and talked a little too plainly to "My Aunt" about what "My Uncle" had been doing, so when he too came home he wrung the bird's neck. It is a Russian version of the fable of the "Goose which laid the Golden Eggs," and is really a very sad little story.

The evening ended when the proprietor finally closed the café, and his patrons staggered away in the dark. Piotr was clinging affectionately to his new friend, who was kindly helping him to carry his equipment and the balalaika. Every little while they had to stop while Piotr unwound his long thin legs which had a tiresome tendency to become entangled with each other.

"Where—where are we going?"

"To a place where we can get another drink," said Zolbin. "Nice place—never turn people out in the dark."

"Very unkind, turn out in the dark. Let's have another drink———"

11 SPOTS WITH TAILS

The two M.V.D. men, Ivanovich and Andreyevich, gave up the search for Zolbin and returned to the Russian sector of Berlin. They were not unduly anxious; most probably Zolbin would break back for the Russian sector and be there before them. It was a little odd the way he had run from them when they had called him by his name, but no doubt he had had an evening full of alarms and was naturally in a state of nerves and disinclined to trust anyone, especially in the Western sector.

"In fact," said Ivanovich, "he did quite right to run from us. He did not know us." In which belief, of course, he was quite mistaken.

"We were, actually, ill-advised to call to him."

"Yes. It only alarmed him the more. I think, Vassily, we need not report that little incident. He will be at police headquarters in the morning."

"I agree, Andrei Ivanovich. In the meantime——"

"Bed. We are both fatigued. Bed."

So they said nothing at Police Headquarters in East Berlin, except that they had arrived on duty and wanted beds for the night. They were allotted a small attic bedroom in an hotel and retired thankfully to rest.

But the next morning there was no sign of Vadim Zolbin anywhere, he had not reported his arrival to the police or applied anywhere for accommodation.

"Where has he gone?" asked Andreyevich uneasily.

"He has returned to the Western sector to carry out his mission and will shortly return," said Ivanovich with a confidence which sounded a little hollow. "He will have to apply to the police to get his return travel passes stamped before leaving for home; if we are patient we shall see him walk in."

But the whole day passed without sight or news of Vadim Zolbin. In the meantime, at the prison in Minsk where Lachmann was confined, the governor had become really frightened because Lachmann's personal papers had not come back. Zolbin had promised that they should be returned in an hour or two and now they had been missing for two whole days. On the second night the governor could not sleep for anxiety and in the morning he rang up a higher authority and reported the matter.

Moscow, always distrustful of Zolbin, took notice at once. What, this notoriously unreliable person had possessed himself of German papers? Let his rooms be searched and his office also, especially his office. Let his employees be closely questioned. Let the M.V.D. at Minsk go into action at once.

Natasha Pavlovna, the secretary, turned pale with terror when the M.V.D. men swept through Zolbin's office like a hailstorm. Where were the keys of the safe? *What?* He had taken them with him? The traitor! Anyone who had connived at this abomination——

Duplicate keys were brought, the safe was opened, and the sheets of drawings unrolled. Even to the M.V.D. men who looked vacantly at them they appeared to have been discarded. One even had "Cancelled" written across it and signed V. Zolbin.

"You, here, what's your name? Natasha Pavlovna. What are these sheets?"

"Old ones," she faltered. "Old workings, discarded long ago. Where did you find——"

"Silence! Are these, or are they not, the designs upon which the swine Zolbin was last working?"

"No—oh, no. They are in the safe."

"*These* were in the safe, woman. Now, what did he say to you before he went away——"

So the hunt was up for Vadim Zolbin. It was known that he had arrived at the Ost station in Berlin and passed into the Western sector in accordance with instructions, but where was he now? He must be discovered and arrested at all costs, dead or alive but preferably alive, and with him some designs which he had stolen from the aircraft works at Minsk. These were very important; if he were caught and they were not in his possession every effort must be made to induce him to tell what he had done with them. He was carrying German papers made out in the name of one Gustav Renzow and when last seen was dressed in a blue serge suit, a striped shirt with a white collar, a blue tie with a pattern of tiny red squares woven in the material—particulars supplied by one Natasha Pavlovna—a grey felt hat, and black shoes.

These particulars were telephoned from Minsk to the

114

commandant of the M.V.D. office in the Eastern sector of Berlin, a pursy little man with the thin, pointed nose of the naturally inquisitive, and sharp eyes behind strong gold-framed glasses. He sent out immediate orders to the police that checks were to be established on all main roads in the Eastern sector and also upon the underground trains, to bring in a tall dark man probably carrying German papers in the name of Renzow and dressed in a blue suit, etc., etc. This was in the late evening of the day after Zolbin's escape from jail and subsequent meeting with the soldier Piotr and his balalaika.

The check upon the underground brought in almost immediate results; less than two hours after the order had been given the East German police arrived at the M.V.D. office supporting the wilting form of a tall, thin dark man wearing a blue suit, a blue tie with small red squares, and so forth. He was carrying the personal papers of Gustav Renzow and had been arrested in the train on his way to the Western sector. The M.V.D. commandant was naturally delighted and ordered that the prisoner be brought before him. When this was done it was immediately plain that the prisoner was suffering from one of the most colossal hangovers in history. He did not appear to take in what was said to him, he could hardly speak in reply, and his eyes did not appear to focus upon the commandant at all. They wandered vaguely round the walls and once fixed themselves so intently on a spot above the commandant's head that he looked round sharply to see what was there, but saw only a blank wall. The prisoner was seeing bright spots which slid away when he looked round at them, he had been seeing them for some hours, but since coming into the brightly lit office they appeared to have acquired tails. The fact was that Zolbin had overdone the amount of drink he had given Piotr and underdone, so to speak, the quality; that last pint of potato spirit had brought the soldier to the brink of delirium tremens.

"Stand him there!" barked the commandant. "Leave him!"

The police obeyed, but the prisoner bent at the knees like a debutante at court and had to be supported or he would have fallen. He closed his eyes against the insufferable light and said that his head ached.

"With respect, Comrade Commandant," said one of the warders, "he is suffering from the aftereffects of drink."

"Sober him, then," said the commandant.

"I am sober," said the prisoner weakly. "I just don't feel well."

"You scoundrel," thundered the commandant, "you are Vadim Zolbin."

"No. That isn't right."

"Don't lie to me! You are Vadim Zolbin."

"No."

Asked what his name was, he could not remember. The commandant laughed scornfully.

"You are Vadim Zolbin."

This time the prisoner did not even trouble to deny it. This interview seemed to have gone on for hours and probably was just another dream; if he took no notice it would go away.

"Where are the papers?"

"What?"

"Where are the papers?"

"What papers?"

"The designs."

The prisoner gave it up again and one of the M.V.D. men hit him.

"Where are the designs?"

"Never had any. What are they? But I've lost my balalaika."

He spoke the thick Russian of the northern provinces and the commandant recognized it; also he knew that Zolbin was an educated man brought up in Moscow.

"This is an act he is putting on," he said, "but I must say he is doing it very well. He looks so stupid, too, but he cannot deceive me. You, Zolbin——"

But the prisoner was fingering the edge of his jacket. "Not right," he said. "Where's my uniform?"

116

"Where are the papers?"

The prisoner focussed his eyes upon the commandant. "The question is," he said carefully, "where is my balalaika?" He then retired into an almost visible cloud of Nordic gloom, and they could get no more out of him.

"Take him away," said the commandant. "He can talk in the morning." The prisoner was hustled out, and the commandant rang up Moscow to report that, in less than two hours after receiving their orders, he had captured the traitor Vadim Zolbin.

"And the papers he was carrying?"

"He has not got them with him now, but he will tell us where they are."

"See to it," said Moscow. "Those two M.V.D. men who were told off to keep an eye on him, what are they playing at?"

"Not my section," said the commandant, "but I will get into touch with them in the morning."

Actually, he had not heard anything about them but he rang up the East Berlin police and was told that there were two M.V.D. men who had been in there asking for news of Zolbin. The ordinary police are a totally different body from the M.V.D. and very often the co-ordination between them is not too good; in any case it was no business of theirs to interfere with men of the M.V.D. who are a law to themselves. But the commandant issued a few brief orders before he went to bed and the result was that when Ivanovich and Andreyevich called at the police station in the morning they were hustled off to the M.V.D. office and given a furious tongue-lashing.

"Moscow rang me up to ask me what you were playing at," roared the commandant. "Why did you not report here? I suppose you were ashamed to admit that you had lost Zolbin. You are right, you ought to be ashamed. When I was asked to find him, I did so at once."

"What?" said Ivanovich feebly.

"I have found your Vadim Zolbin for you. He is here in the cells. He is now going to tell us what he has done with the designs."

117

"Designs? He did buy them then?"

"Buy them?" repeated the commandant. "What are you talking about? He stole them."

Ivanovich's puzzled face slowly cleared. "But how clever of him. Then he won't have to pay for them, will he?"

The commandant turned slowly purple. "Are you drunk too? Will you tell me in plain words what the devil you're talking about?"

"Zolbin," said Ivanovich, "was sent into the Western sector with three hundred thousand Western marks to buy a set of aircraft designs by Gustav Renzow. We were shadowing him but he was arrested by the Wes——"

"Zolbin," interrupted the commandant, "had taken his own aircraft designs from his own office safe at Minsk in order to sell them to the Jewish-plutocratic so-called Western Allies. It is these which he is going to tell us about since he had not got them with him when we picked him up."

"And the money too," said Ivanovich. "Had he got the money on him?"

"About four hundred marks," said the commandant.

"Out of three hundred thousand?" said Ivanovich, and there was an awed silence, broken by Andreyevich.

"No wonder he was drunk," he said thoughtfully.

"I will have him brought in," said the commandant, and gave the order.

The prisoner was brought in, limping because he had been kicked on the knee and was still desperately muddled, blinking because his head ached and the light hurt his eyes. Ivanovich and Andreyevich looked at him, at each other, and back again at the prisoner while the commandant sat back and gloated.

"But this is not Zolbin," said the other two in exact duet.

"Not Zolbin?"

"Certainly not," said Ivanovich firmly. "We know him well. We travelled on the train with him from Minsk; fourteen hours it took."

118

"But it must be Zolbin," said the commandant desperately, for he remembered his vainglorious telephone call to Moscow.

"It isn't our Zolbin," said Andreyevich and added helpfully, "unless it's another man with the same name."

"But he's wearing Zolbin's clothes," argued the commandant, as one fighting a losing battle with fate.

"You," said Ivanovich, addressing the prisoner, who was staring vacantly at the floor, "what's your name?"

The prisoner looked up, remembered what he had been told the night before, and said: "Vadim Zolbin."

"Nonsense," said Ivanovich sharply.

"He said so," protested the prisoner, and pointed at the commandant. "He said it was and I said it wasn't and now I say it was and you say it wasn't. Have it your own way, Comrades." He lost interest again. "My head aches."

"Listen," said the commandant in a quite kindly tone. "It seems a mistake was made last night. Let's forget about that. What is your own name?"

"Vad——"

"No, no," said Ivanovich. "Let me handle this, Comrade Commandant, he seems to be afraid of you." He addressed the prisoner. "Listen to me, and this is going to be quite all right. You've got a home, haven't you?"

"Can I go there?" asked the prisoner, brightening.

"Presently, perhaps. What do they call you when you're at home?"

The prisoner thought for a moment and then said: "Piotr."

"Now we're getting somewhere," said Ivanovich, rubbing his hands together. "I think I'm a good doctor, don't you? Comrade Commandant, can my patient have some coffee, please? Nice strong hot coffee? And permission to sit down?"

The coffee was ordered, the prisoner sat down and appeared inclined to go to sleep.

"Those are certainly Zolbin's clothes," said the commandant. "Look at the tie. Besides, he was carrying

Renzow's papers which Zolbin had. There has been an exchange of clothing, of course."

"And papers, of course," agreed Ivanovich, "since this man has none of his own."

"If we can find out who this man really is," said the commandant, and turned to the prisoner. "Are you a soldier or a worker? Hi, wake up. Are you a soldier, my man, or a worker?"

"Both," said Piotr sleepily. "Who says soldiers don't work?" His head rolled back and he began to snore.

When the coffee came up, the three M.V.D. men found themselves coaxing Piotr to drink it. They had done so little coaxing in their lives that they were not good at it but one cupful went down and half another, when Piotr sat up and looked almost intelligent.

"I'm hungry," he said.

"Bring food," said the commandant, and they sat round and watched Piotr eat bread and sausage and finish the coffee, after which Andreyevich kindly gave him two aspirins.

"Feel better now?" asked Ivanovich, patting Piotr on the shoulder.

"Yes, thank you, Comrade. Where am I?"

"This is the East Berlin Headquarters of the M.V.D.," said the commandant, at which Piotr immediately sprang to his feet and made a bolt for the door. Ivanovich intercepted him.

"It's all right," he said soothingly, "quite all right. Nobody's going to hurt you. Come and sit down again. You have been the innocent victim of a foul plot and we want you to tell us about it. That's all."

"I can't remember anything," said Piotr, addressing himself exclusively to Ivanovich and managing not to look at the commandant. "These are not my clothes."

"What is the last thing you can remember?"

"I was on leave. I came back to Berlin to rejoin—I—where are my papers?"

Eventually, with kindly prompting from Ivanovich who had once been a soldier himself and knew how

120

things are with soldiers, Piotr remembered being in a café with a lot of other soldiers who were all drinking. "I had my balalaika and I sang them the song about 'My Uncle's Parrot.' Do you know it?"

"I do," said Ivanovich, with a smile. "We used to sing it when I was in the Army. What happened next?"

"There was a civilian," said Piotr. "Nice man. He gave me some drinks."

"Where did this happen—where were you?"

Piotr could not remember. "Just a café. I asked a soldier in the street where I could get a drink and he took me in. Don't know its name; never noticed. Don't know where it was, either. I was just strolling about."

"Did you stay there or did you come out later?"

Piotr thought hard. "We came out."

"All the crowd together, or just you and this civilian?"

Piotr shook his head. "Don't know. I remember walking, that's all. Don't know where we went. We had another drink. Don't remember any more."

"And when you woke up, where were you?"

"In a room. I went out and sat in a park. Then I saw these weren't my clothes—I think that's when it was."

"After that, you went on the underground? Why?"

This took a lot of consideration but eventually Piotr's face lit up.

"It was the money," he explained. "Where is it? Western money. I thought, money come from the Western sector, perhaps that's where my uniform's gone. Eh?"

"So you thought you'd go to the Western sector to look for your uniform?"

"That's right. An' my kit an' equipment. An' my balalaika."

"Well," began Ivanovich, addressing the commandant, "there's the story, and personally I believe every word of it. Possibly that last drink was doped, too. Now, the——"

"They brought me here," interrupted Piotr. "All right, bring me here. But why throw me downstairs?"

"That's all right, old man. Nobody threw you, you just

121

fell," said Ivanovich hastily. "Now then. Name, number, rank, section, regiment?"

Piotr reeled them off automatically and the commandant noted them down. Piotr was sent out to sit in another room while further enquiries were made, and the commandant rang up the Army Movement Control. A soldier, particulars given, sent back on duty from leave. Where had he gone? Movement Control said they would look it up and ring back, and the three men waited for it.

"It was, of course, immediately evident to me," said the commandant, "that it was no use enquiring for a missing soldier, since no soldier would apparently be missing. This, of course, was the felon Zolbin's method of getting out of Berlin. I will take quite a large bet that this man was being sent to the Western frontier of the Soviet zone of Germany. Zolbin picked him out from among all those soldiers for that reason."

"You are undoubtedly right in your deduction, Comrade Commandant," said Ivanovich. "Undoubtedly right."

He was perfectly right. Zolbin, faced with the necessity for getting out of Berlin towards the West, had had the brilliant idea of inducing the Army to convey him there with a draft. He had only tripped up over Piotr's untimely arrest, for Zolbin thought that any man with civilian clothes to wear and Western money to spend—hence the four hundred marks in Piotr's pockets—would naturally go astray in Western Berlin for as long as the money lasted and perhaps longer. In the meantime Zolbin would slip off from the draft and it would be days before he was seriously reported missing. Soldiers in all armies have a natural talent for getting lost in transit, rage the transport officers never so furiously.

The telephone rang, and Movement Control said that the soldier in question had been sent off early the previous morning in a mixed draft for the West. His destination was Creutzburg, near Eisenach in Thuringia.

The commandant pulled a map from a bookcase behind him and flung it open on his desk.

"There you are," he said. "What did I tell you?"

The Soviet Occupation boundary was marked by a green line on the map and Creutzburg was practically upon it.

12 CLERICAL DUTIES ONLY

On the following day after the riot at the police station, Hambledon was able to give the West Berlin police a good deal of information about their escaped prisoner. He was one Vadim Zolbin, a Russian. Anything known about him?

A representative of the Political Section nodded. "He's an aircraft designer, he had something to do with the MIG-15. He was trained in Germany, so they say."

Hambledon repeated the gist of the conversation overheard at the café between the two M.V.D. men. "I assume," he added, "that Renzow's designs are still in Berlin and that Zolbin had come, laden with money, to buy them. I may be altogether wrong."

"I should think you're much more likely to be right," said the deputy chief inspector. "And the raid on the police station was an attempt on the part of Gruiter and their friends to rescue the man with the money. Who is left of that gang now?"

"Only Ackermann, of the original four," said Hambledon. "Claussen, Edberg, and Gruiter, in that order, are dead. No doubt Ackermann has other friends, but if we're right in assuming Renzow's designs to be still in Berlin, probably only Ackermann knows where they are."

"And whatever else was taken from Renzow's safe," said Spelmann. "The Pastolsky jewels, possibly."

"Ackermann is being hunted," said the deputy chief inspector. "He is hiding up somewhere; he hasn't been home. We know, now, where he lives."

"If I'd murdered a sergeant and shot up an inspector," said Tommy Hambledon, "I'd never go home again. I take it you have searched his place?"

"Early this morning," said the inspector. "We found a nice ruby ring in a box under the floor boards, nothing else, and his wife didn't seem to know anything or didn't dare to talk."

"May we have a look round?" asked Hambledon, including Spelmann with a gesture. "We might at least find a nice pair of diamond cuff links."

They received permission and that evening searched Ackermann's room after the Intelligence Service manner which involves dissecting everything into its component parts. Mrs. Ackermann sat in a corner, weeping, and Hambledon was sorry for her, but she would not talk and they found nothing. The place was kept under observation but it was difficult to watch; originally the semi-basement of a large department store, the big rooms had been subdivided to accommodate as many families as possible and passages ran all ways with rooms opening off them upon either hand. There were no less than five entrances to this rabbit warren; besides these, several rooms which were immediately within the outer walls had doors of their own. Hans Ackermann's was one of these, and its door led out upon what had been a loadingyard for delivery vans. Two constables did their best to watch the front entrances, while one at the back kept a reasonably attentive eye to a gap in a wooden fence round the yard.

Late in the evening one of the constables in the front thought he saw Ackermann slip through little groups of people going home to bed. He signalled to his colleague and together, with hands on their guns, they followed down the stairs and along the angular passages. They came to Ackermann's door only to find it bolted, they hammered upon it, demanding admittance, but the door remained shut and it took them some time to break it in.

In the meantime the constable on duty at the back saw Ackermann's door open and someone come out. The yard was badly lit and it was not until the figure came towards him that he recognized it as Ackermann with a gun in his hand.

Constable Schultz had not long been in the force, his nerves were not what they had been before the war, and his left ear was still in adhesive bandages on account of a ricochet from one of Ackermann's shots at the police station. This sort of thing, he felt, was not what he had joined the police for; steady pay, a warm uniform, and good prospects, but not battle and bloodshed. Here was a dangerous criminal coming at him with a gun and for a moment he was stiff with terror. However, Ackermann stopped and appeared in the dim light to be looking down. The constable drew his gun, slipped off the safety catch, and rested his quivering hand on the board fence. Ackerman stooped over something on the ground and the constable's finger jerked upon the trigger. There was a loud crack and a bullet sailed over the criminal's head to break a pane in Mrs. Ackermann's kitchen window.

Ackermann was off like an Olympic runner; for a heavy man he could run surprisingly fast. He vaulted the board fence and was away in the darkness before the two constables inside the building, who had heard the shot, could break through into the yard.

Constable Schultz was not the recipient of congratulations, but Hambledon found his story of enough interest to take Spelmann to meet the constable on the spot.

"He stopped in the middle there somewhere," said Schultz, from Ackermann's back door. "I couldn't rightly say just where."

"Where were you?" asked Hambledon briskly. "Over beyond the fence there, I see. Well, we'll go over there and try a little experiment. Spelmann, you are the nefarious Hans Ackermann. Stand in that doorway till I call you on."

Hambledon and Constable Schultz crossed the yard, knee-deep in coarse weed and rough with rubble, and climbed the fence.

"Were you just here?"

"No, mein Herr, I think not quite. A little further round."

"I want you to take me to the exact spot, if possible. Do you think you would know it again?"

"Oh, the exact spot," said the constable, moving on. "I think so. I was sitting on a beer crate."

More stumbling over loose brickbats and the constable stopped.

"I think it was here, for this is the beer crate of which I spoke. Yes, this is right, the Herr will see a gap in the fence through which I was looking."

"I see. Spelmann! Come straight towards me here——is that right? More to the left? Bear right, Spelmann."

"I come," said Spelmann, plunging forward. *"Sei verdammt!* There is some loose wire here. I disentangle myself."

"Is he near enough yet?"

"Not yet, mein Herr."

"What were you doing at this time?"

"I draw my automatic, like this, and rest it on the top of the fence."

"Come on, Spelmann. Well, Constable?"

"A little nearer. So! About there."

"Stop, Spelmann."

"Is this where I stoop down?" asked Spelmann, and did so. Immediately there was a loud crack, a bullet sang over his head, and another window pane fell out.

"Hell to you!" said Hambledon, violently addressing the constable. "What the blazes do you think you're doing?"

"Excuse me," said Schultz. "Please, I am very sorry. I was so carried away by the Herr's reconstruction of the scene that I pushed up the safety catch again and the weapon as it were fired itself once more."

Hambledon realized that the broken window was this time not Frau Ackermann's but the family's next door, and consequently the bullet must have missed Spelmann by yards. "You know," said Tommy sternly, "you're not fit to be trusted with firearms. You'll hurt somebody one of these days."

"I know, I know," said the penitent constable, "but, mein Herr, I only joined the force for clerical duties."

126

Hambledon went over the fence to find Spelmann, who had thrown himself flat when the shot was fired and had stayed down.

"Spelmann! You're not hurt, are you?"

"No, no. I have found something, but in falling my torch has gone from me. There is an iron square here; let the Herr look."

Hambledon turned his torch upon an iron manhole lid, such as covers the inspection pits of drains. It was surrounded by weed, but was itself clear.

"Lend a hand, Spelmann."

They heaved it up to reveal a wire running down; at the top it was hooked over the rim. Hambledon pulled it up and there came with it a canister about three feet long by four inches in diameter. It was made from a length of light tin pipe and had a tin lid soldered on at either end and further protected from leakage by being lapped with insulating tape.

When it had been put under a tap for some time, taken back to Hambledon's hotel and opened with a tin opener borrowed from the kitchen, it yielded up three large sheets of tracing linen upon which were drawings of an odd-looking aircraft. Each sheet was signed in the right-hand bottom corner, G. Renzow.

"There now," said Hambledon, "isn't that nice? Dear Hans Ackermann. How helpful he has proved to be in the end, though outwardly more wart hog than angel, and morally pestiferous. Ha! Now we can pack up and go home. I never did care much for Berlin and now I like it less than ever. What's the telephone number of whoever it is one rings up to ask for seats on a westbound aircraft?"

Spelmann told him. "But usually one has to wait days for a vacant seat."

"Then you can sit on my knee. 'Oh, hush thee, my Babie, the time soon will come,' and perhaps there'll be a cancellation tomorrow. How wise was that great man who said: 'Go West, young man, go West.' Hullo. Is that Tempelhof Airport? Thomas Elphinstone Hambledon speaking, parliamentary private secretary to the Ahkoond of Swat. I must have two seats on tomorrow morning's plane for Wahn airport for Bonn. What? No, not 'what,' Swat. Oh, can't I? How tiresome. Yes, I see.. Very well. That will have to do, won't it? No, I don't think I want to go by train, thanks very much. Yes, please. Thank you so much. Oodle-gobbledy. That's Swattish for 'heaven bless your distinguished family.' Good-bye."

"When?" asked Spelmann.

"On Friday, and today's Tuesday. It is true that it's nearly Wednesday morning, but we have two whole days more to spend in this markedly deteriorated dump. However, even that's better than going by train with Stalin's little hopefuls peering at us through the windows. Besides——"

"Who or what," said Spelmann, "is the what-did-you-say of Swat?"

"Nothing. He never was. The traffic clerk, like Weeping Bill, deemed I meant to mock and then suddenly remembered that he'd heard my name before, so it was all right. Spelmann——"

"What?"

"Since we must spend a couple more days here, let us look into something a little odd. Zolbin. Those two Russian M.V.D. men in that café, Ivanovich and Andreyevich, talked as though they were friends of his. They had been told to shadow him, it is true, but with the idea of protecting him. They were going to rescue him from the police station. Yet, when he has been let out by Gruiter and his private army, does Zolbin join his comrades? No. Not though they rush forward with friendly arms outstretched, crying 'Zolbin! Comrade!' He takes one horrified look at them—and he must have seen them quite plainly, Spelmann—and runs like a hare in the opposite direction. I think it must have been he who knocked an elderly Berliner off his bicycle and rode away on it; the victim came into the police station to complain about it just after the raid, you remember. There's something a little odd about a man—I mean Zolbin, not the bicycle's owner—who has two separate

128

sets of people prepared and eager to break into a police station in order to release him, quite independently of each other."

"He was apparently carrying a large sum of money," said Spelmann. "If the sum is large enough——"

"Rescue parties just naturally converge upon it like iron filings to a magnet. Yes, I see that, but I still think it's a little odd. Why did he run away from his boy friends?"

"Perhaps he was allergic to revolver shots."

"I don't blame him. I am myself. But still——"

"I see one thing very plainly," said Spelmann, laughing. "You want to look into the Zolbin affair and nothing shall stop you."

"I don't want to do anything daring or desperate," said Hambledon, a little apologetically. "I only thought that with a suitable change of clothing and some quite impeccable papers we might just pop over into the Soviet sector and make one or two trivial enquiries. Your official friends here can supply some nice impeccable papers, can't they?"

"Beautiful," said Spelmann enthusiastically, "beautiful. If you wish, we can do that. To pass into the Soviet sector, it is easy; hundreds of people do it every day. We shall not find anything but it does not matter, it will help to pass the time. I will go to the head office in the morning for some papers while you go round the second-hand clothes shops and get some appropriate clothing. Boots particularly, old, cracked, patched boots. I take Size 10½; they may as well fit. We shall at least get some vodka."

The Soviet Government of Eastern Berlin must be quite well aware that very many of its apparently loyal citizens are informing the Western Allies about events, conditions, rumours, and acidly witty stories current in the Soviet sector. Not only are these helpful persons to be found among those who live there, but also among those who pass the Sector boundaries upon their lawful occasions or even upon occasions not lawful at all. You

129

cannot effectively divide a city, and the attempt so to divide Berlin must be one of the silliest efforts in history. Our grandchildren will laugh themselves sick when they read about it.

Hambledon and Spelmann had, therefore, no difficulty in passing into the Soviet sector—they merely went by underground railway—or in finding people who were prepared to talk to them when they got there, but there seemed to be no news of any startling interest. They strolled about, drank some indifferent vodka, had a bad meal in a restaurant, stared into shopwindows which, compared with those in the Western sector, ached with emptiness like a hungry stomach, and returned in the late evening by the underground. They expected no more difficulty than they had had in the afternoon and were horrified when the train stopped at a station right on the sectional boundary and raucous voices bellowed: "All out! All out! Passengers all out, please."

The passengers, including Hambledon and Spelmann, obediently rose and began to file out of the train. The platform was a long one and the train had stopped at the beginning of it. Halfway along the platform a temporary barrier had been put up with a man at either side of it to scrutinize papers as the people passed through two abreast. When the train was empty it moved along the platform to the far end so that those who had passed the barrier and wished to travel further could re-enter the train. Some of the first through the barrier were already hurrying to do so.

"If this reception has been prepared for us," said Spelmann in a low tone, "we may find ourselves spending the short remainder of our lives in an uranium mine."

"Let's nip across the footbridge and get into an east-bound train back into the sector," said Hambledon. "There are other ways out. Oh no, they've thought of that, there's a guard on the footbridge. There's nothing for it but to go on and bluff it out. You said our papers were beautiful, didn't you?"

However, when they came in their turn to the barrier their papers were merely glanced at and returned with a brief *"Danke,"* and they were hustled on to make room for the next victims.

"This is all very odd," said Hambledon, withdrawing Spelmann from the main stream of passengers. "Let's stand here a few minutes and see the fun. Have a cigar."

They lit cigars since, in Berlin, they are the same price as cigarettes and much more satisfying, and strolled about. Almost before the last stragglers from the first train had passed the barrier a second train drew to a stop and the performance went on.

"They are looking for one particular person," said Spelmann, "who is expected to try to get out of the Russian sector. Look, they're not worrying about the eastbound trains."

"Must be somebody important," said Tommy. "Look at all the police hotching round and those flat-faced thugs in a bunch there are M.V.D. men."

Spelmann nodded, the second train pulled past them to resume its passengers, and very soon a third train came in, for this was the rush hour. Towards the end of this train's complement of passengers there came a tall man wandering rather than walking, he strayed uncertainly up to the barrier, bumped into the end of it, and was spoken to sharply. His papers were taken from him and unfolded.

The examiner uttered a cry of triumph and held the papers over his head and immediately police and M.V.D. men closed in upon the tall man. Somebody behind Spelmann shouted something and the examiner shouted back. "That's right. Zolbin."

Hambledon and Spelmann looked at each other and retired into an angle of a bookstall to be out of the way. The prisoner was hurried past them by men holding him by the arms; he was dressed in a neat blue suit with a collar and tie, but his clothes looked as though he had slept in them. His face was pallid and his eyes half closed, not in terror but as though he were half asleep, and he stumbled in his walk. Hambledon had only seen

Zolbin in the distance, under street lamps, running away from the police station after the riot, and did not doubt the identity. "Poor devil," he said softly. "Drunk, or drugs?"

Spelmann pulled Hambledon close and whispered in his ear. "That's not Zolbin."

"What? Not Zolbin? Are you sure?"

"Perfectly sure. Nothing like him. Except the height. He's much the same height, but otherwise, no. I saw Zolbin plainly when he was arrested; a thin-faced man with a beaky nose. This man's got features like lumps of suet."

"Dear me, how very odd. Well, they think they've got what they want. Anyway, the excitement's all over." In fact, the temporary barriers had been carried away, the police and M.V.D. men had all vanished, and the station was left to its regular staff and a horde of bewildered passengers.

"Let's go up to street level," went on Hambledon. "There may be something more to see."

They went up the long flights of steps, came out upon the street, and joined a queue apathetically waiting for a tram. A few minutes later a black car whirled to a stop at the station entrance and police brought forth the prisoner from the stationmaster's office. They pushed him into the car with a policeman on either side of him and plain-clothes men standing on the running boards, and the car drove off. Private Piotr from Archangel, soldier of the Russian Infantry, was on his way to the M.V.D. office of Eastern Berlin.

13 LOCK-UP

Hambledon took Spelmann by the elbow and steered him in a homeward direction. There had been barricades upon the sector boundaries in the streets but they were being hurriedly cleared away and the home-going crowds surged across without hindrance.

"That fellow who's furnaceman, porter, and general factotum at the M.V.D. office. What's his name?"

"Ditz," said Spelmann. "Ditz."

"What time does he come off duty?"

"Soon after ten o'clock when he's banked up his fires for the night."

Hambledon glanced at his watch. "It's half-past eight now. If we go home and change we can get round to his place about the time he gets home. I am tired of these clothes, they smell of mice."

Ditz had been an avowed Communist before the war. When Germany attacked Russia he went into a concentration camp from which the Russians released him in due course. Out of consideration for his sufferings for The Cause, he was given employment at the M.V.D. office in the Eastern sector although he lived, where he had always lived, in the Western zone. He should have been a happy man, but Communism in practice is not very like Communism in theory as expounded at street corners to the unlettered poor. It was true that the Russians had taken all the wealth from those who once were rich, but the poor were still as poor as ever or even more so, and what had become of all those fabulous fortunes was a question Ditz was too prudent to ask. He worked as hard as he had ever done and for a very low wage; he called his employers "Comrade," but had to jump to it when spoken to just as smartly as if he called them "Sir." He was disappointed and aggrieved; when, therefore, it was suggested to him that useful items of information could add to his income, he agreed. After all he was a German and these Russians, once their Communistic glamour had worn off, were merely adjectival Russians.

Hambledon and Spelmann went to Ditz's house to see him that night and found him finishing his supper. His tactful wife excused herself from the company; she had to be up early, the days were long, she was not so young as she had been, and so forth. She went to bed and the three men settled down before the dying fire.

133

Ditz said that things had been pretty quiet in the M.V.D. office for a week or more until tonight when there was a little excitement. Apparently orders had been received that a man named Zardin or something——

"Er—Zolbin?"

"Zolbin, that's right. Zolbin." He was trying to get to the Western sector and was to be captured at all costs. "Must have been important; they put on the whole show for him. Our boss was fair hopping, and when they brought in this Zolbin our boss was that delighted he didn't know what to take for it."

"Did you see the prisoner?"

"Oh, yes. I saw him when they brought him in in our bulletproof Mercedes, and again when they chucked him in the cell. I don't know what he'd had," said Ditz with something like awe in his voice, "but I've never in all my life seen a bloke with such an 'angover. Mister, his eyes was going all ways."

"What are they doing with him, do you know?"

"Nothing, tonight. He was so far gone they couldn't get nothing out of him, one of our boys told me. Oh, and one thing they was all laughing about. This Zolbin, there was two M.V.D. men came with him from wherever he came from and they lost him. Lost him! Swanky headquarters blokes from Moscow or somewhere, and they go and lose him. Our boss is having 'em in in the morning, and I bet he don't offer 'em a bunch of lovely flowers. I wish I could be in the room to 'ear it all, but they'll tell me. They always tells old Ditz, the boys do. Harmless, that's what I am." He tittered.

"Well, listen," said Hambledon. "If anything interesting happens about Zolbin in the morning, could you let us know at once?"

"At once. What exactly do you mean, at once?"

"As soon as the excitement's over, whenever that is."

Ditz looked thoughtful. "I don't get home till late, as you know, and I won't be seen talking to you where I goes for my pint midday. A passing word 'ud be all right if carefully done, but not a long talk if you get me. Tell you what I could do; I could 'ave one of my attacks."

"Attacks?"

" 'Eart." Ditz laid his hand over his heart. "My old ticker ain't too good and I do get attacks sometimes. They don't last, but when I do have one—ach! I suppose they'll finish me one of these days."

"But what happens when you have an attack?"

"They sends me 'ome for the rest of the day. They're pretty good like that; they knows there's no one else can manage them old boilers like I can. Mister, they come out of the Ark. I know how to 'umour them, see?"

"Very well," said Hambledon, getting to his feet. "If anything should happen which you think would interest us, you'll come home, will you? Ring this number," said Hambledon, writing his hotel telephone number upon a scrap of paper, "and we'll come down here and see you. All right?"

"All right, providing you makes it worth my while."

"Don't worry, that'll be all right too."

As they walked away from the house Spelmann remarked mildly that the Herr Ditz was not really an admirable type.

"The typical paid informer," said Hambledon. "Why? Does it matter?"

"I feel I want a bath after talking to a creature like that."

"My dear Spelmann! You wait," said Hambledon with sudden passion, "you wait until you feel like that when you see your own face in the glass."

Spelmann opened his mouth to answer, glanced at the grim face beside him, and held his peace.

Early in the afternoon of the next day Ditz rang up the hotel from a call box in the Western sector on his way home. He said merely that he would be at home that afternoon and hung up the receiver without awaiting a reply. Hambledon went alone this time. Spelmann was at Police Headquarters in consultation about quite another matter.

Hambledon heard a confused story of how the arrested Zolbin had turned out not to be the Zolbin they wanted at all but someone else. The story naturally came as no surprise to Hambledon, but he did not say so. The M.V.D. commandant was no end cast down, according to Ditz, especially after the remarks he had addressed to the two M.V.D. officers from Moscow or somewhere, they who had lost Zolbin originally. Apparently he had swapped clothes with a soldier and it was this soldier who was caught.

"I suppose," said Tommy, "that the two Headquarters men were pretty cock-a-hoop about it all."

"Well, no. 'Course, they scored off the commandant and that's a thing doesn't happen every day, but it don't help them with Moscow, do it? Their man's still lost."

"What are they doing about it, do you know?"

"Going off after him. I was off-loading coke when they come out and I 'eard 'em say as they must catch him or else. And the other says yes, and if they don't catch him it'll be better to keep going straight on themselves. No sense in coming back, he says."

"Oh, really. But what is all this fuss about?"

"They was asking the first one—the soldier—where he'd put some papers. He'd stolen them, it seems."

"Stolen them? But Zolbin never got them at all. I know all about those papers."

Ditz stared. "But I heard the boys saying he'd taken his own designs from his office and skipped with them over to the Western sector. Then he got chased out of there back into the Russian sector, so he changed clothes with the soldier and skipped again."

This, about Zolbin's own designs, was a piece of real news to Hambledon.

"Any idea where he's gone?"

"Now, where would he go, mister?"

"I meant, to which part of the frontier?"

"No idea. Nor where the two Moscow blokes have gone, either."

"Have gone already?"

"Are going, then. And you don't catch me asking neither."

Hambledon returned to find Spelmann waiting for him and told him the news. "Zolbin is quite a star in his line, isn't he? I think somebody ought to do something about all this. I mean, those designs of his ought to interest us."

Spelmann nodded. "If those two M.V.D. men haven't started yet it should be possible to find out where they are going."

Hambledon picked up his hat and started for the door. "I'll go and see my people here, they'll find out."

Accordingly, enquiries were set afoot to find out where and when Andrei Ivanovich and Vassily Andreyevich of the M.V.D. were going. It was already known where they lodged and the rest was easy. They were handed on from one casual loiterer to another when they left their hotel the following morning, carrying their small suitcases. When they entered the Friedrichstrasse station there was yet another man studying a timetable near enough to the ticket office to hear what they said. He waited about the station long enough to make sure that they really had gone away by train and then returned to report. Hambledon received the news by telephone half an hour later.

"They went on the ten-fifteen from Friedrichstrasse station for Eisenach."

"Oh, did they," said Hambledon. "Eisenach in Thuringia, beyond Erfurt. Close to the zonal frontier."

"That's right. About ten miles from the frontier."

"Thank you very much indeed," said Tommy. "You are worth every penny of my income tax."

"Impossible," said the voice, and rang off.

Spelmann, summoned by a page from a *bier-keller* two doors away, came to Hambledon's room to find him studying a railway timetable and packing shaving kit, pyjamas, and a couple of clean collars into a brief case.

"We are going to Eisenach," he said, "on the train which leaves the Friedrichstrasse station at fourteen min-

137

utes past thirteen hours. Andrei and Vassily have started already, but I didn't want to travel with them. They saw us in that café when we were sitting at the next table and they ought to remember our distinguished features."

"They had a good look at us," nodded Spelmann. "Also, I remember, you said you were leaving for Cologne next day en route for Paris. They might remember that, too."

"They will reach Eisenach at twenty minutes past twenty hours," said Hambledon. "At least, so says the timetable. In actual fact, I expect they'll be lucky if they get there by midnight. We're supposed to arrive at twenty-one twenty-six."

"We shall probably be in good time for breakfast," said Spelmann resignedly. "What about personal papers?"

"Those we had the other day will do. Building accessories are likely to be wanted even in Thuringia. What were you, brewery fittings? That'll do, too. I must get a German suit, I fear. See you in half an hour."

The boy called Frett had been taken to Cologne by a friend of Hambledon's and accepted provisionally as page boy by the Kolnerhof Hotel. Here he was well fed and clothed and could have as many baths as he wanted. When the novelty of frequent washings wore off he was no more enthusiastic about them than is any other normal boy of fourteen. He was also kept firmly in order, along with his fellow *chasseurs,* since page boys of all races are just naturally young imps if not wisely restrained. He attended night school four nights a week, he worked hard and was considered promising, and his red head flitted like a flame along the hotel passages at the hall porter's cry of *"Chass'!"*

Five days after the riot at the Berlin police station, the same day as that on which Hambledon and Spelmann were travelling to Eisenach, Frett was spending his afternoon off wandering idly round the Dom Square at Cologne when he saw a man whom he recognized, one of the few people he knew whom he never wished to see again. Frett dodged behind the arcading of the corner shop opposite the main entrance of the railway station and watched Ackermann cross the tramlines towards the west end of the Cathedral.

"What's he here for?" muttered Frett. "No good, I'll be bound."

Frett followed at a distance, employing all the detective tactics he had learned at the cinema, but Ackermann scarcely looked round. He did not know anyone in Cologne and it did not occur to him that anyone there might know him. He walked slowly and steadily across the front of the Cathedral and on up the Hohestrasse, occasionally stopping to look into shopwindows. He was quietly and respectably dressed and attracted no attention. About halfway up the Hohestrasse he turned right into an area of cleared ruins, where Frett had to take advantage of all the cover available to watch him without being seen.

There was a wide road here which had been cleared, its original granite setts still showing the fan-shaped patterns in which they had been laid. There were no buildings of any size here, but some enterprising person had taken advantage of a large flat area of concrete to build lockup garages. They went round three sides of an oblong space; upon the fourth side were large double doors. There was a rough but strongly built wall round the lockups which were, in fact, built against it, and there was barbed wire on the top of the wall to discourage any who might think of climbing over it. Frett knew the place well; it was one of his duties to guide motoring guests of the Kolnerhof to this place if they wished to garage their cars in safety.

Ackermann slowed to a loitering pace and even stopped to stare about like one who looks for some familiar landmark now missing, but it was plain to Frett that his main interest was in the lockup garages. The double doors were wide open as they always were from eight in the morning till midnight, and the man in charge was sweeping the yard and stacking empty oilcans, wooden boxes, and similar debris tidily together at the far end to await removal.

Frett was peering from behind a contractor's hut when someone on the other side, whom he could not see, began to cough; a dreadful rattling cough of a kind which the boy had heard often enough before. Tuberculosis is common among the ill-housed and undernourished, even if they have not been in a concentration camp. Ackermann continued to hang about and the consumptive went on coughing until a neighbouring clock chimed a quarter to six, alarming Frett, who was due on duty again at six o'clock until midnight. However, at this point Ackermann, having apparently seen enough, walked quickly away and Frett dared not take time off to follow him. Frett did decide that it would not take a moment to have a look at the cougher on the other side of the hut so he circled round it and glanced at the man in passing. He saw a young man, thin to emaciation with great hollows below high Slav cheekbones and the heavy "frontal bar of Beethoven"; Frett did not know him at all, but Spelmann would have recognized him at once, for it was the younger Karas, once footman to the princely family of Pastolsky.

Frett rushed back to the hotel, washed hurriedly, hurled himself into his uniform, and arrived in the hall as the clock struck six, only to be sent back by the porter because the thick red hair had been inadequately brushed. Karas stayed where he was, watching proceedings at the lockup garage until it got dark, when he went away to eat hot sausage and drink hot coffee. He came back again later for he wanted to know what happened when the place closed for the night, if it did close at any regular hour. He had been watching the place for three days, "casing the joint," in the English thieves' argot; it took him some time to learn all he wanted to know, for he was not a burglar by profession and this was, in fact, his first attempt. He did not notice Ackermann and would not have recognized him if he had;

140

Gruiter and Edberg he had known, but from Ackermann he had been mercifully withheld.

Late that night, after half-past eleven, there came to the Kolnerhof a traveller desiring accommodation—for the night and a garage for his brand-new Jaguar. His cases were unloaded by the porter and Frett was sent with the motorist to pilot him to the lockups. Frett sat, very smart and upright, in the front seat beside the driver; as the long car turned this way and that to get a straight run in through the big doors, the headlights lit up two lurking figures in different patches of shadow nearby; one was Ackermann, the other Karas, and Frett's sharp eyes saw them both.

"That's queer," he said to himself, "both watchin' this place earlier and both still 'ere."

He nipped out of the car as it stopped in the yard to open the driver's door for him. The garage attendant came forward, and the motorist addressed him in German with a strong English accent.

"I'm awfully sorry," he said, " 'fraid I'm rather late. Can you find room for my 'bus, do you think?"

The attendant said pleasantly that the Herr was by no means too late. "It still wants a quarter of an hour to midnight when I close and now I can go away at once for you are taking my last vacant lockup." He opened a pair of doors, admiring the Jaguar as he did so. *Was für eine schöne auto!* We must take great care not to scrape her. Back once more, mein Herr, and then forward slowly. So-o-o!"

While this was going on, Frett stood unnoticed behind the car, biting his fingers and asking himself what the Herr Hambledon would do under these interesting circumstances, for Frett assumed Hambledon to be a sort of super-detective whom even the police obeyed. Here was one of the criminals for whom his hero had been searching. Would a real feller such as Frett wished to be go tamely home and leave him loose? Never, never. He knew he would have little chance if Ackermann saw him in the open and his spine crept at the thought of

141

Ackie and the things he did to people. What would a sensible man do? Conceal himself, of course, and collect evidence, for he was sure Ackermann had designs upon one of the cars. At this point his eye fell upon the collection of empty oilcans and boxes, now a sizeable barricade.

The Jaguar was eased into the vacant lockup, the doors were padlocked, and the key given to the motorist who paused on his way out and looked round the yard.

"The Herr desires——" began the attendant, who wanted to get home.

"Nothing, thanks. I only wondered where that boy had gone to."

"Cut off back to the hotel, I expect. Them young imps, they can't wait a minute."

"They're generally patient when there's a tip in the offing. Never mind, no doubt I shall see him in the morning."

His footsteps retreated and there followed the squeak-bump of the big doors being shut and the sound of a key being turned. Silence and loneliness settled upon the yard until a red head arose from behind the oilcans.

"I think I'm a fool," said Frett forlornly, "an' if something don't happen I look like getting the sack out of this. I could climb them gates, but what it'd do to my new uniform——"

14 SLEEP WELL, SOLDIER

A long five minutes passed, and Frett was beginning to creep out on a tour of inspection when a sound at the yard gates sent him scurrying back to cover. An arm appeared over the gate followed by the rest of a man's body, the man got over the top and dropped down inside to lean panting against the door trying to strangle a fit of coughing.

"Poor old Bellows-to-mend," commented Frett.

Karas pulled himself together, picked up a satchel he

had dropped over the gate when he climbed it, and came along the yard peering at the numbers painted on the lockup doors. He found the one he sought in the middle of the row on Frett's right, took out a hacksaw from his satchel, and began to saw through the hasp of the padlock.

"Car stealers," muttered Frett disgustedly. "Car stealers, that's all and not even one from our 'otel at that. I shan't half get the bird for this."

Karas was not very expert and the light was bad. He broke a saw blade and went over towards the gates, where the light was better, to replace it. Frett's impatience rose to fever point. There were three tradesmen's delivery vans parked in the open, to be taken out early in the morning. They were on the opposite side of the yard from the busy Karas and Frett wondered whether he could creep along behind them and be over the gate and away before—— The padlock fell with a rattle and Karas pulled open the lockup doors. He went inside. A car door opened and closed again and presently the car itself came out backwards with Karas pushing it. He turned the steering wheel with a hand through the window and the vehicle backed round towards Frett and his barricade. The car was a Citroën and bore the insignia of the French Army headquarters staff. Disaster seemed imminent when Karas snatched at the brake and stopped the car. After a moment's rest he took the brake off again and began to push the Citroën forward towards the yard doors.

This was harder work still; Karas struggled gamely, but the task was plainly beyond his powers. While he was still heaving painfully, Frett's attention was distracted by the sight of another man coming over the gate, a bigger man this time and much more athletic. He dropped noiselessly to the ground and came running on silent feet round the yard behind the parked vans. The boy recognized him with horror for this was Ackermann: Frett shrank away and made himself small in the darkest shadow of the furthest corner, while Ackermann came on to hide, in his turn, behind the same range of empties but some ten feet away.

Karas neither saw nor heard anything, for his blood was thumping in his ears and perspiration running into his eyes. Suddenly he abandoned the attempt and leaned heavily against the car, clinging to the door handle and gasping for breath. Ackermann crept out and as he went Frett saw him draw something from his left sleeve, something thin and pliable and heavy at the end. He crept up behind Karas, rose to his full height, and struck with all his strength at the defenceless head. There was a dull, hard thud and Karas fell to the ground to lie there, not even twitching.

Ackermann stepped unconcernedly over his body and opened the off side of the bonnet. Frett had a boy's interest in cars and this saloon was of a common type, a Citroën such as are seen by the thousand on Continental roads; he could follow quite easily what Ackermann was doing. He was checking over the car for its running condition, the petrol supply, the oil and water level, the presence or otherwise of the rotor arm. The clicks were clearly audible as the distributor head was sprung off and replaced. Frett knew about rotor arms; a tiny part, indeed, but without it no car will go.

Ackermann left the bonnet open—probably he wanted to flood the carburetor at the last moment—and went across the yard to the gates where he busied himself with the lock upon the wide doors. Frett, quaking but audacious, crept out and slipped round the Citroën to the bonnet. Karas had left the car slewed across at an angle and the open bonnet concealed the boy from the man at the gate. Frett removed the distributor head, taking particular care that the spring should not click this time, drew out the rotor arm, and replaced the head with even more care. A dozen silent strides across the yard took him behind the nearest of the parked vans; he dodged in the shadow from one to the other just as Ackermann had done when he first came in, and waited there, quivering with excitement, until the gates were

144

opened wide and hooked back and Ackermann returned to start the Citroën.

Frett was out of the gates in a moment and running like a hare. It was another landmark in his career that for the first time in his life he was actually seeking a policeman. He rounded a corner and ran straight into the arms of an extra large one. The arms closed about him.

"Mister," began Frett, "what's it worth to——"

He stopped. This was not the way to talk now; he had left all that behind in Berlin.

"What's worth what?"

"I say, d'you want promotion? There's a man broke into the lockups there tryin' to steal a car."

"Now then——"

"Besides," gasped Frett, "he's committed a murder."

"Nonsense! If you think I've——"

"Listen!"

There came clearly to their ears the whine of a self-starter. Not a hearty whine but a hesitant one; evidently the battery was down. The policeman released Frett and strode purposefully towards the sound. Frett paused only to drag a short but heavy length of iron bar from a heap of rubbish they were passing at the moment, and trotted after him. The policeman saw that the yard gates, which should have been shut, were indeed open and lengthened his stride. When they entered the yard, Ackermann was half in and half out of the car fumbling in the dark for the starting handle but without success. He heard footsteps and looked round.

Frett hung back; the policeman was young and strong, but Ackie was still Ackie. Ackermann made to get out his gun but the policeman sprang at him and the battle raged over the yard between the vans, round the Citroën, and over the body of Karas. They fell into a clinch, grunting and straining, and Frett saw his chance; he danced up behind Ackermann and hammered him over the head with the iron bar. Ackermann staggered, the policeman hit him hard under the jaw and knocked him out.

145

After that it was simple. The policeman blew his whistle for reinforcements which arrived at a gallop. Ackermann's arms were handcuffed behind him and he was left to await police transport summoned by telephone.

"Here's the corpse," said Frett with assumed calm, but his voice ran up in a squeak.

"Take it easy, boy," said his first friend. "You haven't done too badly tonight."

"That other man," said Frett, struggling to control his teeth, which were beginning to chatter, "is Ackie from Berlin. Ackermann, he's horrible. You won't let him go, will you?"

"No. Oh, dear me, no. He's finished. Look, you come from the Kolnerhof, I see. I'll walk along there with you."

"Th—thank you," stammered Frett. "And will you p-please t-tell them I haven't been in m-mischief? I don't want to get the sack," and to his rage and disgust large tears began to roll down his face.

"You come on," said the policeman. "You're all right. What you're suffering from is shock. You want a nice nip of brandy and off to bed. I'll talk to the Kolnerhof."

Zolbin, in Piotr's uniform, with Piotr's papers and carrying all his equipment except the balalaika which Zolbin presented to his landlady, went to the place of assembly for troops being drafted to the West. He knew where to go and at what time, for all this was written upon Piotr's leave pass. He entered the barrack square where the transport waited, there were many other men like himself straggling in in loose groups and he attracted no notice. The transport officers were bustling about glancing at each man's place of destination and rounding them up into groups for the different vehicles. Zolbin was hustled into a lorry with benches down either side; there was not enough room on the benches for all the passengers so the last comers sat on the floor. It was very early in the morning, a little after four o'clock, the men were chilly, sleepy and dispirited; when the last man was aboard and the lorry jolted into motion most

146

of them wriggled into the most comfortable position attainable and tried to go to sleep. It is about two hundred miles from Berlin to Eisenbach. As soon as the lorry came out upon the great Autobahn it settled down to a steady thirty-five miles an hour and the monotonous road slid past. They stopped for a meal at midday; thick soup, bread, and potatoes; in half an hour they were away again but the hot meal and the short break had awakened Zolbin's companions and they began to talk. What worried and alarmed Zolbin was that he had practically no notion of what they were talking about; soldiers' slang is baffling to the civilian. He decided that he had better keep quiet but even this was not easy, they were friendly souls and they tried without success to draw him out.

"You're one of the silent ones," said one of them, "aren't you, Comrade?"

Zolbin made an effort. "I'm sorry, Comrades, to be so dull. The fact is that while I was home on leave my wife died. Please let me alone, Comrades."

After that they left him alone. The day passed slowly and they arrived at Eisenach towards five in the evening. They climbed stiffly down from the lorry and stood about, stamping their feet and stretching their cramped limbs while a sergeant scanned their papers and sorted them out. Zolbin and six others were ordered back into the lorry to be taken the half-dozen miles on to Creutzburg.

"When you get there," said the sergeant, "you'll find someone to tell you where to go."

"I expect so," said one of the six. "That's one thing that's never failed me in the Army yet, somebody to tell me where to go."

"None of your lip," said the sergeant. "Drive on!"

They drove on to Creutzburg and once more climbed out of the lorry into, more or less, the arms of yet another sergeant. Three of the party remained in Creutzburg; the other four, including Zolbin, were told to go on down a road which the sergeant pointed out.

"You," he said to Zolbin, "take the first on the left

and keep on till you come to a wood. There is a lane through the wood. Turn right down it. There is a cross-roads less than a kilometre down the lane. Turn left and in ten minutes you'll be home. Got it? Left, right, and then left; just like marching. You three, keep straight on till you reach the road post and there you are. About five kilometres. Go on, march!"

They did, but Zolbin bungled the regimental movements and covered it by stopping to tie up his bootlace. The other three went on and left him; they found him dull company anyway and he would be turning off in about two hundred yards. Zolbin glanced back but the sergeant had already gone into his office and there was no one about to criticize a soldier's bearing.

Zolbin padded off along the road. He had been used to wearing light shoes; the heavy Army boots with soles like boards hampered him severely, but at last he was alone. He turned left as directed, the frontier must be to-wards his right hand somewhere. He came to a right-hand turn long before the wood and took it, only to run into a patrol of two men coming up.

"Where are you for, Comrade? Let's see your papers. You've turned off too soon. Go on to that wood and turn right there. It's not far now, Comrade."

Zolbin sighed, returned to the road and walked on and on, past the wood, past his turning. The wood ended and there was pasture and arable land. His boots hurt him and his ankles ached. Another patch of wood-land, a bean field, a potato field. It would soon be dark; he would find somewhere to lie up for the night and go on tomorrow. No, go on tonight till he came to a farm and, when they were all asleep, slip in and steal some clothes and especially some more boots. Clop-clop, clop-clop. There was a blister coming on his right heel.

"I know why soldiers are issued with these boots," said Zolbin bitterly. "It is to make it impossible for them to run away."

He plodded on with his eyes on the road and started

148

violently when a voice suddenly addressed him in German from behind a hedge.

"Good evening, Comrade Soldier," it said.

Zolbin stopped and looked up to see a moon-faced yokel with a hoe upon his shoulder looking at him over the hedge.

"Good evening," said Zolbin.

"What are you doing here?"

"Well, come to that, what are you doing?"

"Hoeing," said the yokel, and grinned. "Where's the fancy-dress dance?"

"Fancy-dress dance?"

"That's what I said."

"Why?"

"Because anyone can see you're not a soldier. You don't walk right, you don't hold yourself right, you can't swing your arms, and you can't endure your boots."

"That's true, anyway," said Zolbin impulsively.

"Well, well," said the yokel, and grinned more widely than ever.

Zolbin made up his mind suddenly. "Is a hundred marks any good to you?"

"Money always looks good to me. What for?"

"Civilian clothes instead of these."

"Soldier," said the yokel, "for another two hundred marks I'll hide you, too."

Zolbin hesitated, but he might go much further and find nothing better. He had to trust some stranger, he knew no one in these parts. He shifted his feet and the blister on his heel gave him a stab of agony which settled his doubts.

"Very well. Thank you. Where do we go?"

"Just a bit further on there's a gate."

Zolbin limped along the road and his new friend kept pace with him inside the hedge. The gate admitted Zolbin to a rutted dusty track across fields and they walked along it together, the yokel occasionally swinging his hoe round his head in a manner which made the Russian acutely uneasy.

"Where are we going?"

"To the farm, of course. By the way, I'll have the first hundred marks now."

"Certainly," said Zolbin. He took some notes from a pocket in which he was carrying a few for immediate expenses and gave the yokel two fifty-mark notes which were promptly stowed away. "To the farm," continued Zolbin. "But won't the farmer object?"

"He won't find you if you're lucky, and if he does he won't dare say anything. It's him as would get into trouble for harbouring you, not me. He'll keep quiet for his own sake. See?"

"But doesn't anybody ever come here?"

"No. Use your head," said the yokel contemptuously. "What would anyone come here for?"

He waved his hoe again and Zolbin looked wearily round an empty landscape of gently rolling country with large open fields, few roads, and still fewer buildings of any kind. The yokel began to laugh to himself and Zolbin asked him sharply what the joke was.

"Funny, that's all. Here's us two walking along together, you pretending to be a soldier and me pretending to be a farm labourer."

"And aren't you?"

"Not really. It's convenient for the moment, same as you. It's only when I look at my hands." He held them out. "I tell you, when I get a pack of cards in my hands again I shan't be able to feel them. It's all this *verdammlich* hoeing. How I hate it!"

For he was, in spite of his bucolic appearance, a cardsharper. His round face with its silly, good-tempered expression, and his look of country innocence had helped him enormously in taking money off city men who think themselves so much cleverer than the rustic. Even when he won mysteriously and unexpectedly, it was hard to believe that he had done it, as it were, on purpose. That gap-toothed grin and the childlike yells of delighted laughter when he fumbled his cards and produced an unexpected ace, surely behind them there could be no guile. However, he had got into trouble and the Russians were not amused. Hitler's jails were bad enough but the Soviet ones were worse; worse still were the uranium mines to which he was assigned on his third conviction. He slipped off the train, went into hiding, and acquired a set of false papers. Since quite twenty per cent of the Germans in Soviet-occupied Germany carry false papers it follows that they are not very difficult to get, but his stated that he was a farm labourer, so a farm labourer he had to be. It was better than the uranium mines and would not last so long if he could help it. Only till next harvest when the farmer had sold his produce and brought home the money. Then, if all went well, the farm hand would disappear and the money too.

The farm came into sight; a solidly built Thuringian house with a big square of farm buildings behind it, barns and cowsheds and piggeries, cart sheds and stables.

"Is the farmer at home now?" asked Zolbin nervously.

"Not he. He's been to monthly market to trade a bit and pick up the usual bunch of new regulations for farmers. How to get more eggs on less feed. He'll get drunk; he always does whenever he gets a new set of regulations. Mister, he wouldn't see you tonight if you danced round him in pink satin tights. But keep out of his way tomorrow; hangovers don't agree with him. This way."

Zolbin was led into a vast barn and up a steep ladder to a half-empty hayloft. Trusses of hay were pulled out to let him crawl in behind upon a bed of hay softer than any mattress he had ever slept upon. He pulled off his boots, and that in itself was bliss.

"Got any matches?" asked the farm hand.

"Yes—why?"

"Hand over. Can't run any risk of you smoking in here."

"I'm not a fool——"

"Never mind. Nor am I. Hand 'em out."

Zolbin obeyed.

"That's right. You go to sleep and I'll bring you

something to eat in the morning. Sleep well, soldier, sleep well!"

The last thing which Zolbin heard for nearly twelve hours was the sound of heavy boots descending the ladder.

15 THE BLACK CROSS

Hambledon and Spelmann arrived at Eisenach some time in the small hours of the morning. Not wishing to make themselves conspicuous by wandering about empty streets in the middle of the night, they lay down on benches in the waiting room and dozed uneasily until morning. When the town was thoroughly awake they arose, stiff, unrefreshed, and hungry, and went out to find breakfast.

"I should like to know," said Hambledon, pulling his hat down over his eyes, "where Andrei and dear Vassily are staying."

"We needn't worry just yet," said Spelmann. "They also had a long journey yesterday and Russians don't like getting up early. It is not yet half-past seven, they won't be about until ten at earliest."

They went into a café which was only open in the sense that the doors and windows were standing wide and vigorous cleaning operations were in progress. The operator was a young German with an artificial foot and three fingers missing from his left hand, but he was mopping the floor with scalding hot water and a long-handled mop while a young woman moved tables out of his way which had plainly only just been scrubbed. The place was poor and cheap, but clean.

"Excuse me," said Hambledon. "I'm afraid we're horribly early, but is there any chance of breakfast?"

"In a quarter of an hour," said the young woman, "we shall be having ours while these tables are drying. If the Herren could bear to wait——"

"Could we not help?" asked Spelmann. "Tell me, mein

152

Herr, how you want these tables moved and let me take the place of the *Würdige* Frau for this morning."

"So that you may get your breakfast earlier?" smiled the German. "It will be a help, we are a little behindhand this morning."

"We overslept," said his wife, and abandoned the tables and chairs for her kitchen at the back. Hambledon found himself dusting chairs and polishing the inevitable mirrors, while Spelmann and the proprietor straightened up the café. A quarter of an hour later the woman came back to ask if the Herren would care to breakfast with them in the kitchen, it was pleasanter in there. They sat down at a scrubbed deal table to coffee and hot rye bread and ate hungrily. The young woman said that they had taken over that business when Rudi came back from the war too disabled to work on a farm any longer; it was a poor living but one could manage, and there was the house to live in also. The ground floor only, of course, the upper rooms were tenanted by another family. "Nice people, Germans like ourselves, elderly but kind. The good Frau was most kind when our Margrethe was born last year."

At that point our Margrethe announced her presence, awake in the next room, by a series of healthy yells, and the mother excused herself and left the table.

"The Herren are making a visit to Eisenach?" said Rudi.

"A short visit," said Hambledon. "We are travellers in builders' fittings and we have some calls to make."

"Is this your first visit to Eisenach? Yes? Perhaps I could direct you to wherever you wish to go?"

"You are most kind. The first thing I want to know," said Hambledon deliberately, "is whether there is an M.V.D. office in this place and, if so, where it is."

There was complete silence for a moment and the German dropped his eyes. When he looked up again all the friendliness had gone from his manner and his voice was cold and formal.

"There is not, I believe, actually an M.V.D. office here.

153

There is, however, the Police Headquarters to which I will direct the Herren if they wish——"

"To avoid it, *um Gottes willen!*" said Hambledon emphatically. "There are two M.V.D. men who came here yesterday by an earlier train than ours. They saw us in Berlin and we would rather they did not see us here."

The German's face cleared slowly.

"I had not heard that they have come," he said, "but I am not surprised. There is some sort of an upset here about someone who, they say, has got away, or is trying to get away. Some say it is a soldier who has deserted, but they would not stop all leave, man all the emergency road posts, and double the patrols just for a deserting soldier, surely? Myself, I know nothing and do not ask, but you know how gossip flies round. If the Occupying Power"—he snarled the words—"has its troubles, I fear we Germans tend to be merely amused."

"You do not happen to know anything about the deserting soldier, by any chance?"

"Oh," said the German slowly. "Oh, really. No, I'm afraid I do not, but I might be able to put you in touch with someone who does. Is the deserting soldier, then," he added with a sly smile, "interested in builders' materials?"

"He might be, don't you think?" said Hambledon. "If he has left the Army he will want somewhere to live, poor man, won't he?"

They all laughed and the German said that a cousin of his kept a small newspaper shop in Brückestrasse, on the righthand side just before the bridge. "He is a good man and reliable. He has, of course, to serve all who come, but he is none the less trustworthy. He hears all the news."

"Being a news agent, naturally."

"Naturally. One moment."

The café proprietor went across to a desk, took from it an empty envelope addressed to himself, and signed "Rudi" across the corner of it. "Give him that and he

154

will know you come from me; it will save time. I am sorry to be so—what is the word—conspiratorial? But we live in curious times."

"Heaven send us a speedy end to them," said Spelmann.

"A happy end," the German corrected him. "Some ends might be worse than our present case and at least we live."

Hambledon and Spelmann took a cordial leave of Rudi, his wife, and of our Margrethe who clutched at Spelmann's hair, and made their way to the news agent in Brückestrasse. He was a wizened little man whose right arm was missing from the shoulder, but his eyes were bright and interested in all who came. He had some customers, among them two Russian soldiers, so Hambledon and Spelmann looked at picture postcards till the coast was clear and only then handed Rudi's envelope across the counter.

The news agent looked at it, crushed it in his hand, and said that perhaps the gracious Herren would honour his sitting room by entering it. He lifted the flap of the counter and they passed through into a small room behind the shop where, before doing anything else, the news agent dropped the envelope into the fire.

"One cannot be too careful," he said. "Will the Herren take a cup of coffee?"

"Thank you," said Hambledon, "but we have just this moment had breakfast with your cousin and his charming wife. I do not wish to take up your time——"

The shop bell rang, the news agent said: "Excuse me," and went into the shop. He served a customer and returned.

"In what way can I serve you?"

"Your cousin said that there had been some upset about a deserting soldier and he thought you might know a little more about it than he does."

The shopkeeper's eyebrows went up. "There is something a little unusual about that deserter," he said. "They say he is only a private; all I can say is that they must

155

be getting uncommonly short of privates and of that I see no sign as yet." The shop bell rang. "Excuse me."

When he came back again Hambledon asked if the deserter had disappeared from Eisenach.

"No. Oh, no. Though emissaries came round to all the shops in the town yesterday asking if any of us had served such a one, describing him. As though we ever troubled to distinguish one from another! A Russian uniform, that is enough. One looks no further. No, it appears he came to this place with a mixed draft of soldiers most of whom stayed here, but he, with a few others, was sent on to Creutzburg. He did not join his unit and that is all I know."

"Creutzburg," said Hambledon.

"About six miles. Across the bridge, across the Autobahn, and straight on. There is a bus."

"We will patronize the bus, I think. When we get to Creutzburg——"

"There is an old man, very fat, very infirm. He suffers with his legs and walks with two sticks. I say, walks. He does not walk, he sits all day on a bench outside a tavern called der Schwartz Kreutz down by the river. Turn left from the main road by the bridge this side of the river. His name is Wilhelm Treiber and he was for many years the local policeman there. He knows all the people and their parents and their grandparents. He likes beer." The shop bell rang. "Excuse me."

When he came back he said: "Tell him Gerard sent you and ask after his yellow hen. I gave her to him and sometimes she lays an egg."

"Splendid," said Hambledon. "I am immensely grateful to you. Where does the bus go from?"

"The post office in the square. Wait just a moment, it would be as well if you were not seen coming out from this room. Excuse me." He went into the shop and the next moment called to them. "Come now."

They went out just in time, the counter flap had barely closed behind them when another customer came in. Hambledon and Spelmann nodded to the news agent and went out. The square was within sight and there was a bus standing outside the post office; a single-deck country bus with people climbing in. They made a rush for it, seeing that Creutzburg was on the destination board, and then had to wait on the pavement while a fat woman with three grandchildren, four bundles, and a basket was hoisted on board. While they stood there two men came out from the post office, passed close by, and saw Hambledon and Spelmann in plain view. The two men paused in their stride and there came over their faces that where-have-I-seen-that-man-before look which is quite unmistakable.

The fat woman squeezed through the bus doorway with an almost audible pop, Hambledon and Spelmann leapt in after her, and the bus moved off, leaving Ivanovich and Andreyevich on the pavement staring after it.

"That was a bit of bad luck," said Spelmann softly.

"Can't be helped," answered Hambledon. "We shall have to be extra careful, that's all."

The bus lumbered on. At the point where their road passed under the great Autobahn from Dresden, they were stopped by a road post and all their papers examined before they were allowed to go on. The bus stopped, naturally, a good many times; usually at side turnings. Hambledon noticed that there was a road post round each of these turnings though the bus was not halted again by the Russians until it reached Creutzburg.

"They are being very industrious this morning," said a fat man with a pipe. "Does anyone know what all the fuss is about?"

"Does anyone care?" said a thin-faced man with an acid expression, probably due to gastric ulcers.

"It is said—I cannot say if it is true—it is said that they have lost one of their soldiers," said the fat woman with the bundles.

The driver looked over his shoulder. "Must be more than that. They have plenty more where they come from."

"Perhaps one of them has lost a watch," suggested Hambledon, and everyone laughed. The Russian passion

157

for watches and clocks is still a joke among Germans.

"So long as they do not accuse us of murdering him," said the thin man.

"Or of stealing the watch," said the fat one. He was sitting across the gangway from Hambledon and Spelmann; he leaned towards them and said: "The Herren are from the Rhineland?"

"That is so," said Spelmann. "The Herr can tell by our speech, no doubt."

"That is so. I also came from the Rhineland many years ago, many years. I was born at Boppard on the Rhine; my father kept an inn there. *Ach, so!*" He looked about him, the fat woman with grandchildren and bundles occupied the seats behind while in front were people whom he obviously knew. "These Russians," he said, dropping his voice. "I was told a story by an English officer in Berlin about the early days before the Russians separated themselves. There was a Russian officer came into the mess where this British officer was, with others, and the Russian was carrying a washing basket," he gestured, "you know? It was full of things he had looted from houses; nothing would stop the Russians from looting. One of the things was a kitchen mincing machine. You know? It has a handle by which you turn the insides. The Russian wound the handle and nothing happened, so he said: 'No music,' and threw the thing out of the window." The fat man shook with laughter. "A mincing machine and he thought it a musical box."

"The British officer," said Hambledon, "should have told him to put his finger in and then wind the handle. There might have been some music then."

"That is so—he should——"

The bus stopped in the village street of Creutzburg and Russian soldiers solemnly went through all the papers again, after which the passengers got out and went their separate ways. At the bottom of the sloping street there was a bridge in plain view; Hambledon and Spelmann, spared the necessity of asking for it, walked straight on towards it and turned left before crossing the bridge.

158

Only a grassy bank, with goats tethered upon it, lay between the road and the river; on the left were small houses, a cobbler's shop, and the inn of the Black Cross. It was very old; a timbered building with steep gables, standing a little back from the road with a magnificent chestnut tree on the green before it. On either side of the inn door there were benches against the wall and upon one of these an enormously fat man was sitting with two sticks propped up beside him; even as they drew near he picked up a beer pot from the table before him and drained from it what were evidently the last few drops it contained.

Hambledon and Spelmann strolled up to the door, greeted the old man, and said the day was hot, with the Herr's permission they would join him in the shade. He lowered his head a little, which was the nearest he could get to a bow, and waved his hand in a welcoming manner. They sat down and the landlord came out of the doorway and looked at them.

"Beer, please," said Hambledon, "for myself and my friend. And the Herr here—if he will honour us——"

The old man ducked his head again and said: "Beer. I thank you," in a surprisingly deep voice and the innkeeper retired. They sat in silence, looking at the river and the green fields on the further side, until the beer came when they said: *"Prosit"* to each other and drank contentedly.

After a time, Hambledon said: "Forgive a stranger if he is, perhaps, mistaken, but do I address the Herr Wilhelm Treiber?"

"You do," said the ex-policeman, and swivelled round upon his seat to face Hambledon more directly. "Everyone in these parts knows old Treiber."

"I was talking this morning to someone who said that he knew you. I was to say that Gerard sent me and to ask about the welfare of the yellow hen."

Treiber nodded his head slowly. "The yellow hen is well and even laid an egg this morning which my little

159

grandchild ate. Gerard keeps a news agent's shop in Brückestrasse, Eisenach."

"And has lost his right arm."

"In the Ardennes," agreed Treiber.

Credentials having been established, Hambledon took a long pull at his beer, which was better than might have been expected, and said that Gerard thought Treiber might be able to tell him—Hambledon—something about a deserter whose absence from duty seemed to be worrying the Russians.

Treiber thought it over for some minutes and then said that he did not know anything personal about this deserter, but that anyone who managed to worry the Russians to this extent was worthy, in his opinion, of encouragement. "But I do not know even his name. I regret."

"I myself," said Hambledon, "do not know the name under which he is passing at the moment."

"Passing at the moment," repeated Treiber. He emptied his pot of beer and looked thoughtfully into it, Spelmann did the same. Hambledon took the hint, tapping his pot on the table, and the innkeeper came to the door and looked at them.

"Three more, please."

"I do not ask," said Treiber firmly. "It is a mistake, in these days, to know more than one need. Does the Herr know him?"

"I should recognize him," said Spelmann. The innkeeper came out with the fresh supply; when he had gone again Spelmann added: "I am an officer of the Security Police at Bonn."

"I am honoured," said Treiber, lifting his pot. *"Gesundheit!"*

"Gesundheit!"

"Gesundheit!"

"As for this deserter," said Treiber, reverting suddenly to the official police manner of his earlier days, "it is reported that he was returning from leave to a small detachment posted in that wood which you can see over there at the top of that rise. It is called the Markgraf's

Planting and is larger than it appears from here, it runs down the other side of the ridge for nearly six kilometres. It runs toward the frontier," he added.

"Yes?" said Tommy.

"He did not join his unit in the wood. From what you say, it is clear that he had a good reason for not joining them since I assume that he was travelling under some other soldier's name."

"That is right," said Spelmann. "He made the soldier drunk in Berlin and took his uniform and papers."

"So he would naturally not let the soldier's comrades see him," said Treiber. "He went along the road towards the wood and did not turn down into it, he kept straight on. My informant, who was preparing to lay a few snares, was not to be seen, but he saw the deserter march on along the road. He—my informant—said that he did not believe the man was really a soldier, he had not the bearing. Even such bearing as these Russians have." Treiber attended to his beer for a moment. "Also, my informant thought him a townsman, for why did he not leave the road? Marching along for everyone to see!"

"Did anyone see him after that?"

"I have not actually heard that anyone did so but I do not get about much, as you can see. My legs. I have to sit here and wait for information to come to me. But there is a man who, if that deserter kept on walking along that road, would certainly see him."

"And who is he?"

"Paul Treiber. He has the same name as I but we are no relation, there are many Treibers in Creutzburg. He and I are the same age; we were at school together, but he is not afflicted like me. No, he is active and strong for his age though bent, very bent. Almost double. He is a roadman; his job is to cut back the hedges and keep the ditches clear. He lives in a small cottage beside the road some three kilometres beyond the Markgraf's Planting. When he is not working on the road he is sitting at his window looking out."

While Treiber was speaking, a car passed along the

road. Hambledon, who was leaning forward with his elbows on his knees, did not look up, but Spelmann's eyes followed it. There was a small pennon on the bonnet to proclaim that it was on official business.

"I think," said Hambledon, "that we cannot do better than walk along and have a word with Herr Paul Treiber."

"You cross the bridge," said Wilhelm Treiber, "and the road is the first turning on the left, quite near. Less than two hundred metres. But there is a road post at the turn today, so they tell me. If the Herren climb over a gate just upon the other side of the bridge, they will find a track across a field which cuts off a corner and brings them out on the road near the Markgraf's Planting."

Spelmann got up. "The advice is so excellent that I think we ought to follow it at once."

Hambledon was so accustomed to Spelmann's bursts of energy that he did not hurry. "Tell me," he said to Treiber, "how much of all this about the deserter do the Russians know?"

"How can I tell? We do not talk to them, but they may have seen him themselves." To Spelmann he added: "That was only the police car from Eisenach."

"I thought it might be," said Spelmann, and fidgeted from one foot to the other like a dog who is tired of waiting.

"Oh, was it," said Hambledon energetically. "Here, Herr Innkeeper! *Die Rechnung, bitte?*"

Hambledon paid the man, he and Spelmann shook Treiber warmly but hastily by the hand, and they left the Black Cross inn with long strides.

"I didn't notice the car," admitted Hambledon. "Careless of me. Did you see who was in it?"

"A passing glimpse," said Spelmann, "but it was enough."

"Did they look at us?"

"I could not say. At least, they did not stop."

"No. Nor will we, I think. Here's the gate, over!"

Andrei Ivanovich and Vassily Andreyevich did recognize Hambledon and Spelmann in Eisenach as the two who had sat at the next table to theirs in the Berlin café when they were discussing how to rescue Zolbin from the police station.

"It is odd," said Ivanovich, "that those two should be here, and going to Creutzburg."

"Why?" asked Andreyevich. "Businessmen do travel about in search of orders, do they not? More so in these disorganized Western parts than is done with us. I have read articles about the custom."

"Of course you did not understand, as I did, what they were saying at the next table. The taller one said that he was going back to Cologne the next day."

"Perhaps his seat on the aircraft was taken from him for some important person. Or something occurred to prevent him from leaving. Or perhaps he received other orders."

It will be remembered that the Russians had not seen Hambledon and Spelmann outside the police station at the time of the riot and had no reason to suspect them of any interest in Zolbin, but Ivanovich was suspicious by nature and training.

"I still think it a little odd," he said doubtfully. "We will keep a look out for them."

"Coincidence," said Andreyevich soothingly. "Coincidence."

When their car passed the Black Cross inn they were hurrying to a hamlet a few miles downstream from Creutzburg because a report had come in that a man had been arrested there who might be Zolbin. As they passed the inn Ivanovich said: "There are those men again."

"We cannot stop now, Andrei Ivanovich."

"No. But we might do so on the way back."

The prisoner was nothing like Zolbin so on the way

back the car stopped at the Black Cross and the Russians got out. Old Treiber sat unmoved as they walked up to the house and the innkeeper came to the door and looked at them.

"Those two men who were here half an hour ago—who were they?"

"Inspectors," said Treiber.

"Inspectors," said the innkeeper.

"Inspectors of what?" asked Ivanovich.

"Beer," said Treiber, and the innkeeper nodded.

"Their names?"

"Muller," said Treiber, "and——" He glanced at the innkeeper.

"Mahler."

Ivanovich noted down both names and then returned to their car with Andreyevich close behind. The car drove off. Treiber continued to stare into vacancy and the innkeeper went indoors again without another word.

Hambledon and Spelmann walked on and on, through the Markgraf's Planting and out the other side. They did not keep to the road as Zolbin had done before them; there were tracks through the wood parallel with the road and they used these; when they left the wood behind they walked inside the hedges whenever possible. Nearly two miles beyond the wood they came to a stretch where the ditches had recently been cleaned out, round the next corner they found a bent old man working upon them.

"Excuse me," said Hambledon, "do I address the Herr Paul Treiber?"

The old man leaned upon his shovel.

"You do."

"Herr Wilhelm Treiber, at the Black Cross, sent us to you. He thought you might be able to tell us something."

"What is that, mein Herr?"

Hambledon explained, and Paul Treiber said that he had, indeed, seen the soldier pass on that day. "He was limping, mein Herr, his right foot hurt him."

"You did not see where he went?"

"The last I saw of him, he was talking to Farmer Hagen's labourer down the road there."

"And then?"

"When I looked again they was both gone. I didn't see him no more, nor I didn't hear his boots on the road no more."

Hambledon asked where Hagen's farm was and received directions for finding it. He thanked the roadman and was in the act of moving off when Treiber stopped him.

"Old wreck, ain't he?"

"Who?"

"Wilhelm Treiber. Never think we was the same age, would you?"

"Well, no, perhaps not," said Hambledon, who had taken a liking to Wilhelm Treiber.

"Reckon I'll outlast he," cackled the old man, and turned to his work again.

Hambledon and Spelmann walked on to the gate through which Zolbin had passed two days earlier and took the same fieldpath which he had taken. The Russians had not neglected to search the neighbouring farms for the fugitive, they had searched Hagen's very thoroughly the day before Hambledon went there. They did not find Zolbin, who was lying flat on one of the great beams high up in the roof of the barn and had to stay there until the farmhand came back with a ladder in the evening. Hagen, who did not know that he had a visitor, was furiously angry, but it is of no use being angry with Russians, they take no notice.

When Hambledon and Spelmann drew near the farm they heard the intermittent bursts of explosions such as are caused by someone trying to start, with a handle, a small stationary engine which does not wish to keep running. The farmer had dug a new well and acquired a motor pump to bring up the water; his old well, which had run dry, was being filled in by degrees. The farmer did not drive a car and was not in any sense a mechanic; the pump was exasperating him. When two strangers walked into the yard the farmer lost his temper completely.

"What the hell do you want? Can I have no peace on my own place?"

"We are inspectors from the Ministry of Farm Production," began Hambledon, but the farmer cut him short. He told them what, in his opinion, they were and that they could be more usefully employed in applying natural fertilizer to the fields. He said that it would be better still if they themselves became that natural fertilizer except for the risk of their poisoning the crops. He then seized the starting handle and wound it with such violence that the terrified engine awoke and ran as it were for its life. Slightly appeased, the farmer told Hambledon and Spelmann to go where they liked and count the hens' tail feathers if they liked, so long as they were off his premises before he returned. He then dragged his hat down on his head with both hands by the brim and departed with angry strides towards the horizon.

"Something seems to have annoyed him," said Hambledon mildly.

"I shouldn't think he's hiding Zolbin," said Spelmann, "would you? He doesn't seem to mind us hunting round. At least, I mean, he did not attempt to prevent us."

"No, that's true. But Zolbin might be here and he not know it. Besides, I want a word with that farm labourer."

They walked round the farm and found no one about except an old peasant woman peeling potatoes in the kitchen. When they spoke to her she merely shook her head, pointed to her ears, and said: "I can't hear," in the high toneless voice of the totally deaf. They went out again, looked into sheds all round the yard, and finally came to the big barn.

"There's a hayloft above," said Spelmann, when they had peered round reapers, binders, rollers, and other agricultural machinery.

Zolbin was sitting in a bare space on the floor of the loft since hay is warm stuff to lie in and it was unbearably hot up there under the roof. He heard two men below speaking German, it was a little less alarming than men speaking Russian but not much. He turned on his knees and tried to crawl silently across the floor to hide again in the hay, but Hambledon's quick ears caught a sound of movement. He held up a finger to Spelmann and pointed upwards. Spelmann nodded.

"I wish we could find that farmhand," he said clearly. "Then he could take word to Herr Zolbin that we've come to get him out or tell us where he's gone."

"He might not believe you," said Hambledon.

"I could show him my Bonn police card," said Spelmann. He stopped speaking and they listened, but there was no sound from overhead.

"I'll just go up the ladder and look," added Spelmann. "We can't hang about here all day."

He went slowly up the ladder. "Herr Zolbin! Is the Herr Zolbin there? We are friends from the Western zone."

He put his head above floor level and saw Zolbin standing a few feet away with a long-handled axe in his hand.

"At last!" said Spelmann. "Herr Zolbin, I know you though you do not know me. Heinrich Spelmann of the Bonn Security Police. We have followed you from Berlin to get you out. Do you know the M.V.D. are here?"

"Here?" said Zolbin hoarsely, and the whites showed all round the iris of his eyes.

"Not on this farm, not yet. In Creutzburg."

"I thought that as this farm was searched yesterday, I should be safe today. How did you find me? If you could, they can."

"Not necessarily. We are Germans, people talk to us who will not talk to the Russians."

Spelmann could not know that four fields away a police car was drawn up at the side of the road while two M.V.D. men interrogated a bent old man who was clearing out a ditch.

"Did two strangers in civilian clothes come along here half an hour ago?"

167

"Haven't seen any—*ach!*"

"Did two men come along here———"

"Did two men———"

"*Ach!* You hurt me. Yes, they may have done. Yes———"

"Where did they go?"

"How should I know?"

"Where did they go—where did they go—where did they go———"

Zolbin, reassured about Spelmann's intentions, came down the ladder and stood in the barn, talking to them and enjoying a cigar, his smoking having been limited to two cigarettes late at night under the farmhand's supervision.

"I understand that you want to get over into the Western zone," said Tommy.

"I cannot imagine how you learned that, but it is quite true," said Zolbin. "What I really want to do is to get in touch with a man named Renzow, Gustav Renzow, an aircraft designer. He used to live at a place called Königswinter on the Rhine, but I suppose he's in America by now if he's got any sense. I want to talk to him about some aircraft designs."

"If you mean his which were stolen," said Hambledon, "they're quite safe and on their way to him."

"Oh, are they? Good. No, I didn't mean them———"

He broke off and dodged back out of sight of the door as the sound of rumbling wheels came into the yard. Hambledon looked out.

"It's a half-witted-looking farmhand with a cartload of earth."

Zolbin came forward and waved his hand cheerfully to signify that all was well; the cart passed on round the end of the barn and stopped there; sounds of shovelling were then heard above the more distant sound of the motor pump still faithfully running.

"That's Heini and he's anything but half witted, especially where money is concerned. They're digging a pond in one of the fields and he's carting the earth up here to fill in the old well, they were at it all day yesterday. These are his spare clothes I'm wearing; they cost me a hundred marks."

"You were talking about some designs——"

"Oh, yes. Not Renzow's, my own. We've been working on much the same lines and if we could get together——"

"But have you got them with you?"

Zolbin patted his chest where a faded cotton shirt bulged above stained and patched trousers. "Hence my lumpy figure," he said. "The coat hides most of it, but I can't do up the buttons."

"There aren't any," said Hambledon.

"What? Nor are there. I had not noticed that. How are we going to get out?"

"I don't think that will be difficult; we have the sympathy of the local population. Your fellow here could hand you on from one to another. I suppose he was waiting till the hue and cry died down a bit."

"Or till I ran out of money," said Zolbin.

"What? Are you paying him so much per day?"

"A hundred marks."

"No wonder he doesn't want to part with you. Well now, I suggest that you stay here till it gets dark. We'll clear off now and put out a few feelers and get the lie of the land; when we——"

The sunlight darkened in the doorway, and even as Hambledon turned he saw Zolbin and Spelmann put their hands up. He looked round to see the grinning faces of Ivanovich and his assistant above their levelled revolvers.

"Hands up, you also! Or we shoot you. We do not mind." Hambledon obeyed. "I was so sure, if we followed you you would lead us to this traitor here and I was right. A nice haul. Now we pack up and all go home—with me. Vassily, go to the car and get out the handcuffs. I can hold these three heroes. Shut the door after you."

Vassily backed out, shutting the door behind him.

169

"Turn round, all of you. That is right. Walk straight forward towards the wall. Stop. Now you wait."

They stood there waiting while Alexei Ivanovich rejoiced aloud. It was only natural that he should; it had been a long and difficult chase and now he had not only the man he sought but also two villainous emissaries of the Western so-called democracies, and so on. Presently the door opened again.

"Handcuffs, Vassily? Now——"

There was a dull cleaving sound such as in civilized countries is only heard in butchers' shops and a clatter as the revolver fell to the floor. Hambledon spun round to see Ivanovich's body fold up and fall to the ground with Heini the farmhand standing over it. He had split the Russian's head with his shovel.

"There, mister," he said, addressing Zolbin, "and only a thousand marks between friends. Well worth it, ain't it?"

"Where's the other one?" croaked Zolbin.

"Oh, I seen to him, too, when he was bending over the car. Easy. Now, you pick 'em up and drop 'em down the well and I'll go on shovelling. Simple. Then you take the car away and no one'll know they ever come here."

"Where's the car?"

"Round the other side, by the pump engine."

"That's why we didn't hear it," said Spelmann.

"That's why," agreed Heini. "Nor did I. Didn't know there was anyone else here till I see 'em creeping round the barn looking for trouble. D'you want this gun?" He kicked at the revolver which was lying on the floor, and Zolbin picked it up.

"Thank you," said Spelmann, and took it from him.

"But——" said Zolbin.

"You're going into the Western zone," explained Spelmann. "You won't want it there." He dropped it into his own pocket and Heini grinned more widely than ever.

"Are you coming with us?" asked Hambledon.

"No, thank you, mister. I've been in the Western zone."

"Didn't you like it?"

170

"Oh, yes. Fine. But I got into a bit of trouble."

"And you——"

"And there weren't no well 'andy."

"I see," said Hambledon. "Come on, all of you. We'll tidy up before we go."

When the Russians had been bestowed in the half-filled well, Zolbin unbuttoned his shirt and pulled out a roll of notes which made Heini open his eyes very wide indeed.

"If I'd known you'd got all that——" he began.

"I might have gone down the well instead of the Russians?" smiled Zolbin.

"Oh, don't say that," protested Heini. "I've treated you honest, haven't I? But my prices might have gone up a bit."

"They shall," said Zolbin, and gave him fifteen hundred marks. "Will that help you to forget you've ever seen me?"

"Mein Herr, I'll remember you only in my prayers and that's never."

"Splendid," said Hambledon. "Now, where's the car?"

They walked round to where it stood at the further side of the farmhouse within a few yards of the new motor pump, still running.

"Got to build a shed over that before the winter," said Heini, "somebody has."

"Not you?" said Hambledon.

"If I'm still here in four months' time you can take me to have my head seen to."

Spelmann went to the car's bonnet and drew the little pennon out flat between his fingers.

"What does this mean?" he asked Zolbin.

"Official car, let pass."

It was a big car, a Mercedes-Benz, solid and heavy. Hambledon walked across and looked at it.

"Does this mean," pursued Spelmann, "that we can pass all their road posts and patrols?"

"Certainly," said Zolbin. "Everything except a frontier post."

"You're quite wrong," said Hambledon.

"Oh no, I'm not. A frontier post stops everything."

"What, a flimsy piece of quartering hinged to a post at the roadside stop a heavy car like this when it's going fast? Don't be silly," said Hambledon. "Spelmann, you and Zolbin get in the back, I'll drive. Good-bye, Heini. Go and fill up your well before somebody looks into it to see how much work you've done this morning. All set? Well, hold your hats on———"

Gustav Renzow's house stands between road and river; his sitting room looks upon the Rhine and has a verandah outside its windows upon which one may sit to watch the long strings of barges labouring upstream or passing swiftly down. The house is a little outside Königswinter on the Nieder Dollendorf side, but near enough to be able to see, on the left the ferry crossing, crabwise, the strong current to Mehlem on the other side where the great white buildings of the American Headquarters stand among tall trees. Lean forward and look across the river to the right; that huddle of roofs crowned by a round tower on a hill is Bad Godesberg where an English statesman met a German dictator and brought back a fallacious hope and a year's grace. The larger white steamers are the long-distance river boats most of which pass Königswinter by; the smaller white boats, some no bigger than launches, are the short-distance river boats which put in at every little place where there is room for a hinged landing stage and a steep flight of steps up the riverbank. When any boat which is travelling downstream wishes to put in anywhere, her skipper must turn her right round and head upstream to the landing place or she will be swept past. You cannot apply brakes on the Rhine.

There was something like a party in progress upon Herr Renzow's verandah. The aircraft designer himself in an armchair, pallid and weak after his long unconsciousness but wide awake and almost well again; his niece Anna Knipe fussing happily round him; Hambledon, with a tall glass of beer beside him and a cigar be-

172

tween his fingers, looking contentedly across at the wooded hills; Zolbin, thin and nervous but no longer irritable, sitting on the edge of his chair with his eyes on Renzow; and finally Heinrich Spelmann, who had just come in with a paper he had handed to Renzow.

"There is your receipt from the Deutsche Bank in Bonn. Endeavour not to lose it. That scrap of paper represents a large fortune in a small tin trunk, the Pastolsky jewels, mein Herr. They were in the boot of the stolen car, of course."

"Thank you," said Renzow. "Thank you indeed, had it not been for you and the Herr Hambledon I should never have seen or heard of them again."

"Not me," said Tommy Hambledon. "Frett. The boy Frett. You'll do something for him, won't you?"

"I want your advice about that, yes. He should be trained first and then have a business bought for him later on. I understand he wants to be an hotelier in Switzerland."

"Help, no," said Tommy. "Let him train in Switzerland and then take an hotel somewhere else. It's no good roaring in a lion's cage, there's no future in that."

"But tell me, *gnadiges* Fraulein," Spelmann was saying to Anna Knipe, "young Karas, why did he——"

"Oh, the poor boy," she said. "My father found him in a concentration camp dying by inches, he got him out and sent him here. He was dreadfully ill and we nursed him here, not to health, he was too far gone for that, but he did get better. He had a sort of romantic attachment to us; he was always saying he would die to do us a service and so, in the end, he did. Poor Karas, such a nice gentle young man. I remember him perfectly well as a footman at my grandmother's home, years ago, before the war."

Tommy Hambledon's eyebrows shot up before he could stop them, but Anna Knipe noticed nothing. He avoided Spelmann's eyes, but the same picture was in both their minds, of the thing that had been Edberg tied to a chair in a cellar in Berlin. The gentle Karas was probably better dead; he was a little too much like a faithful man-eating tiger.

"Just one more question," said Hambledon, "before we go and let you rest, Herr Renzow. Fraulein Knipe, when you found the jewels were gone, why did you not complain to the police?"

"I was afraid, mein Herr. First, we said nothing about them for fear they should be taken from us and sent back to Poland where the Russians would get them; and then I was afraid to admit they were gone for fear we should be held responsible for their loss."

"But they are yours," argued Spelmann. "There are now, alas, no Pastolskys left and your father was their nearest relative."

"We think so," she said simply, "but will the West German Government think so? And the occupying powers?"

"Certainly," said Spelmann stoutly. "The West German Government is reasonably moral and the occupying powers quite incredibly so."

Everyone laughed except Renzow, who said: "Yes, I know. That is why we were afraid they would send the jewels back to Poland."

"Let me reassure you," said Hambledon drily. "To be incredibly moral it is not really necessary to be incredibly silly also."

THE END